A Longbourn Entanglement

A Comic Pride and Prejudice Variation

MONICA FAIRVIEW

WHITE SOUP PRESS

*For what do we live, but to make sport for our
neighbors, and laugh at them in our turn? —
Jane Austen, Pride and Prejudice*

Chapter 1

*27 November 1811, around eleven
o'clock in the morning*

When Fitzwilliam Darcy woke up, he felt as if he had been trampled by hundreds of sheep. He had counted them as he struggled to get to sleep. If one could grace the way he spent his night with the name 'sleep'. And if the animals that had trampled him were sheep, as opposed to galloping herds of wild horses determined to mow down anyone in their way.

Not that it mattered what metaphor he used for how he was feeling. He knew precisely *why* he felt trampled, and *who* had done the trampling. The figure that came to mind bore little resemblance to a sheep, or to a horse for that matter. It took the form of a charming young lady with unsettling dark eyes and a siren laugh that lured him to set everything in his life aside and follow her.

There was nothing metaphorical about the way Miss Elizabeth Bennet had destroyed his peace of mind and eliminated any possibility of restful sleep. Last night when he had danced with her at the Netherfield ball, he had known with absolute certainty that if he stayed a day longer, he would find it impossible to leave. And leave he must, because duty and position and the weight of centuries of tradition dictated that he could not even consider her a suitable candidate for marriage. It was becoming more and more difficult for rational thought to prevail. Better to leave now, before he was caught like a fish on a reel and left gasping for breath.

Fish and sheep. That was what he was reduced to.

If only he could stop thinking of her! The flash of her dark eyes and the quirk of those seductive lips haunted his nights and days, along with the tinkle of her laughter. The ball last night had left Darcy in a state of fevered agitation. The image of Miss Elizabeth Bennet intruded on his mind, no matter how much he tried to dispel it. No. Not the image. It was more than that. The feel of her as she danced with him. The touch of her fingers through her gloves. The heady scent of her hair as she twirled close to him – a subtle hint of jasmine and soap and something uniquely hers. The mix sent his senses giddying around until he thought he would melt with a need to draw her closer, to crush her to him.

The grandfather clock at the end of the hall

chimed solemnly, a reminder that it was time for action. It was already eleven o'clock. If this was to be his last day at Netherfield, preparations needed to be made for departure. And, most importantly, he needed to make certain that Bingley did not stay behind. Bingley was in just as much danger of being entangled as Darcy was.

Darcy threw aside his covers and dressed himself without ringing for his valet. He could not delay a moment later. He strode down the corridor and rapped at Bingley's door.

"What it is?" said Bingley, sleepily. "Is the house on fire?"

Darcy stepped into the room.

"The house is not on fire, but I know something that is."

"The stables?" said Bingley, sitting up in alarm.

"No. Your heart."

"Oh, is that all?" said Bingley, preparing to slip down under his cover and go back to sleep.

Ruthlessly, Darcy took hold of the cover and pulled it away.

"What the devil, Darcy? What are you up to?"

"I need you to come walking with me."

"Go walking by yourself."

"You will come with me, or I will tell Miss Bingley that you broke that Ming Dynasty vase that she is so proud of."

Bingley groaned.

"Very well, Darcy, but you had better have a good reason to wake me up so early the morning after a ball."

It was a blustery November day, with the wind blowing first from one direction, then from another, and confusing the weathervane – a painted iron cockerel swinging back and forth on top of the house, unable to decide on a direction. The clouds tossed and turned, racing madly one way, then stopping as if meaning to turn back.

In other words, it was a dismal kind of day, but at least it was not raining.

Fitzwilliam Darcy waited impatiently, his back stiff and his mood surly -- to say the least. He had an unpleasant conversation ahead of him – quite literally, since his friend Charles Bingley was leading the way through the gates of Netherfield. He was dashing away, irritated at being forced out of bed into the cold.

Not that Darcy blamed him. Now that they were outside, he realized it was a mistake. He should have spoken to Bingley in the comfort of the manor, sitting by the fire, somewhere where Bingley could not bolt. Darcy had wanted privacy, away from the prying eyes and ears of Bingley's sister Caroline – a young lady for whom eavesdropping was second nature -- but he had not counted on Bingley stalking off.

As it was, Darcy was forced into a jog to catch up.

"We need to talk, Bingley."

Bingley stopped and looked completely unimpressed.

"I have a feeling I know what is going to happen. *You* intend to talk, and *I* am expected to listen to you. And something tells me I know what you are going to say. You are going to repeat what Caroline has been harping on for the last ten days."

It was insulting to be compared in any shape or form with Caroline Bingley, but Darcy was prepared to overlook it. He had more important concerns to discuss.

"Whatever your sister has been harping on is beside the point. I am offering you advice because I have always done so, ever since the first day we met. Have I ever given you bad advice?"

Bingley chuckled. It was a good sign. At least he had recovered from his ill humor.

"I am prepared to acknowledge that your advice *generally* has been good, but you have on occasion been wrong."

Darcy had taken Bingley under his wing when he had been a naïve young boy facing a group of upper-class bullies on his first day at Eton. Darcy had stepped in to defend him then, and he would continue to do so now. The machinations of greedy, matchmaking mothers were just as much of a threat to Bingley as those playground bullies, and Darcy was not about to let any of them win.

"Well, in this case, I am right. You have never lived in a country estate, in a place like Meryton, where everyone knows everyone else. In places like this, you have to be very careful not to arouse false expectations. When there are only four and twenty families, gossip spreads fast. Last night at the ball, I overheard some very alarming insinuations."

It was more than insinuations, but Darcy did not want to sound as if Bingley could no longer back out.

Mrs. Bennet had been crowing to everyone last night that Bingley was as good as engaged to Jane Bennet, and to judge by the other guests, most of the inhabitants of Meryton saw it as a foregone conclusion. If Bingley stayed any longer, he would be honor-bound to propose to her.

A few more days, and it would be too late for Darcy as well, although he could not accuse Miss Elizabeth Bennet of deliberately setting her cap at him. She had flirted with him and laughed with him, but he had detected no hint of artifice in her. Her manners were naturally playful, and she had a charm that could not be learned. That was what had drawn him to her initially. Yet he had never suspected her of artifice. If she had started to occupy his thoughts too often for comfort, he had only himself to blame. He should not have allowed her to bewitch him.

There was only one way to save himself, and that was to establish as much distance between him and her as possible. After a raw night spent imagining Elizabeth Bennet in his arms, he knew it would be disastrous to stay in Meryton even an hour longer.

"You cannot raise the Bennets' expectations, especially since you are perfectly aware that marrying Miss Bennet is out of the question. You are standing at a crossroads, Bingley, and if you do not stop and consider what you are doing, you will take an irreversible step that you will regret for the rest of your life."

"You make it sound like the end of the world, Darcy. I do not see it that way. The Bennets are a respectable family."

"Hardly. With an uncle in Cheapside, it must materially lessen the Bennet sisters' chances of marrying men of any consideration in the world. Think about the implications. Most of your relations will not be gentlemen. It will come to reflect on you, and your children."

"I care not a jot about that."

"But you must," said Darcy, in exasperation. "It will lessen your sister's chances now, and it will hinder your daughters' chances in the future. You have worked hard to be accepted into society. Do not cast it all away for the sake of an infatuation."

"It is not an infatuation," said Bingley, looking stubborn.

Darcy took a deep breath. This would hurt, but

it was essential for his friend to know it.

"You cannot know that, not without giving yourself time. Besides, have you considered that any attachment may be on one side only? I have observed Miss Bennet very carefully, and I have seen no sign of genuine affection for you. Are you willing to sacrifice so much when you will be putting yourself in the hands of a fortune hunter?"

"But she smiles at me," said Bingley. "Her eyes light up whenever I approach her. She shows me a marked preference over all the other gentlemen. I am not mistaken in this."

"Have you never considered that her mama might have instructed her to do so?"

Bingley's shoulders slumped and he turned pale. Darcy shifted his gaze across the fields to Oakham Mount, unwilling to witness the misery on Bingley's face. His friend's unhappiness mirrored his own. They would have to weather the storm together – they would have to stay strong against the temptation to give in to their feelings.

"I know it will be a struggle to regain control," said Darcy, knowing full well what his friend was going through, "but you will prevail, and you will look back at this moment and be glad that you escaped. You cannot stake your future and that of your sisters on a momentary obsession with a young lady who cares nothing for you."

His mind returned to Miss Elizabeth Bennet. Pert, mischievous, and defiant, she was thoroughly beguiling. He was filled with a terrible longing to see her. It tore at his very core. If only circumstances had been different. If only their status was equal.

But they were not, so he had to forget her, come what may. He would do so, and he would help Bingley to accomplish the same.

"I really am sorry, Bingley. I wish it could have been different."

To Bingley, Darcy was the villain in this piece just now. Darcy knew that only too well, but his friend would thank him one day.

"What you say may or may not be true, Darcy. I cannot tell if she cares for me. But is that really the most crucial thing? What if she is only pursuing me because of my money? Is that so very wrong? Does that mean I have no chance at happiness?"

Bingley looked pleadingly at Darcy.

"Do I not deserve that chance? I am twenty-three, Darcy. I am well versed in the ways upper class society works. After all, I have grown up amongst them. I have witnessed firsthand the tricks and in-trigues set up by matchmaking mamas to entrap gentlemen into marriage. That is the way of the world. Many marriages do not involve any affection between the two parties."

He paused and stared out into the distance.

"Everyone knows I am the most impatient of fellows," he continued. "But that does not mean I am utterly reckless. Even if I was, I do care enough about my sister Caroline not to marry on an impulse. I know I have a considerable amount of reflection to do, and I do agree with you that putting some time and distance between Miss Bennet and myself might help me gain a sense of perspective before I become too entangled." He gave Darcy an unsteady smile. "Believe it or not, I do have a brain, and I am capable of working out these things myself. I was actually contemplating going to London this very afternoon."

Darcy let out a huge sigh of relief. Bingley was taking it like a proper gentleman – with an appropriate sense of stoic resignation.

"However," said Bingley, breaking in just as Darcy was about to congratulate him for his good sense. "I warn you. I have not given up on the idea of marrying Miss Bennet. I am only giving myself a chance to ponder the matter more thoroughly."

It *was* too good to be true that Bingley would surrender so easily. However, it was a start. Once in London, Darcy, along with Bingley's sisters, would make sure to keep Bingley caught up in the amusements Town had to offer. It would not be long before he forgot all about Miss Bennet.

"Excellent," said Darcy, confident that the matter was as good as taken care of, "then we had better turn back and begin our arrangements for departure."

Just as they were turning, they heard a shout, and someone came trotting towards them. Darcy squinted against the sunlight to determine who it was. The rider took off his hat and began to wave it frantically.

There was no mistaking his identity. It was his aunt's tedious rector, Collins.

"Hurry, Bingley," said Darcy. "I am in no mood to listen to any more gibberish about my aunt."

Bingley looked doubtful.

"Are you certain? He seems rather determined in his pursuit. If he goes any faster, he might tumble off. It looks as if the wind might knock him down. I have never seen anyone with such a bad seat. Besides, we can't outrun a horse. He will catch up eventually."

Bingley was right. The man looked like he might topple any minute. Much as he despised Collins, Darcy did not want an injury on his conscience.

"Oh, very well," he said, "but I warn you, if he has nothing of importance to say, I will set off at once and leave you to deal with him."

The two men watched as Mr. Collins approached. His clothes were askew, his hair standing on end, and his tricorn hat was crumpled in his hand. Collins' obsequious manner usually induced fury in Darcy, but the sight of him hanging on for dear life was so ridiculous Darcy felt an unexpected impulse to laugh.

"I see you are bravely determined to exercise your horse, Collins, despite the wind," remarked Darcy, striving to keep his expression neutral.

"Not at all, Mr. Darcy, though of course under different circumstances—" He fumbled in his clothes,

13

took out a kerchief and began to mop his brow. "I have come directly from Longbourn. It is a matter of some urgency, but I do not know the way to Meryton. It was most fortuitous that I ran into you, Mr. Darcy. I hope you will point me in the right direction. A most terrible thing has happened."

Any impulse to laugh was replaced with alarm.

Darcy let out an explanation. "What is it, Collins?"

"Has something happened to one of the young ladies?" said Bingley, turning white as a sheet.

"No, they are in perfect health." He gave Bingley a superior smile. "Nothing to worry about on that front. The young ladies engage in exercise daily, and —"

"Mr. Bennet, then?" prompted Darcy impatiently, his mind racing over the implications if Mr. Bennet should fall suddenly ill.

"I know nothing about Mr. Bennet's health. He received a letter last night. An old Oxford friend of his was taken ill. He departed early this morning."

"Mrs. Bennet, then?" said Darcy, gritting his teeth. Would he have to name every single person in the Bennet household before Mr. Collins would provide the information he was seeking?

"How perceptive of you to guess, Mr. Darcy, but I would expect no less from a nephew of Lady Catherine. Alas, Mrs. Bennet has suffered an apoplexy. She is on her deathbed."

Darcy bit back an oath. They had wasted precious time trying to extract information from Mr. Collins, moments better spent fetching the apothecary. What were the Bennets doing, sending a fool like this on such a vital errand? Every moment of delay risked Mrs. Bennet's life. Why had they not sent a man servant? Elizabeth at least should have known better.

Perhaps Miss Elizabeth was in such extreme distress she was unable to think straight.

"I will take care of it," said Darcy. "If you will give me your horse."

"But I—"

"It is best that you return as soon as possible to Longbourn, Mr. Collins," said Darcy. "You may inform the ladies that I will send the apothecary immediately."

"Yes, yes, of course," said Mr. Collins.

As he set off at a gallop, his mind told him it was folly, that he still stood a chance of freeing himself from Elizabeth's influence, and that if he stayed, he may well reach the point of no return.

His heart had other ideas. It leapt at the chance of staying. It sang with joy of relief. It whispered that he could be with Elizabeth when she needed him. In the absence of Mr. Bennet, if something happened to Mrs. Bennet, she would need help. Collins could not be relied upon.

Ultimately, he had no choice. It was, quite simply, the only honorable thing to do.

Chapter 2

27 November 1811, one hour earlier

"**O**h, girls, this is the happiest day of my life. We are saved!"

Mrs. Bennet was waving her hands in excitement. The Bennet girls were all sitting in the morning room, except for Lizzy, who was in the parlor with Mr. Collins.

Lydia snorted. Poor Lizzy, to be married to such a pompous fool! She would rather drown herself than be shackled to such a dismal bore.

She yawned loudly at the very thought of it.

"He should have proposed to *me*," said Mary. "I believe *I* am the most suited to Mr. Collins of all my sisters. Unfortunately, he is too taken in by appearances. The saying goes, 'Do not judge a book by its cover,' but Mr. Collins lacks the discernment to follow this adage. Lizzy will not make him a good wife."

"What is that to the purpose, I should like to know?" said Mrs. Bennet, dismissively. "Lizzy will do her duty and ensure we are not destitute. That is all that matters. When Mr. Bennet dies, Lizzy will become mistress of Longbourn."

Lydia sat up in her chair and stared at her mother.

"What do you mean, Lizzy will become mistress of Longbourn?"

"La, Lydia!" said Kitty, giggling at Lydia's ignorance. "It means that once Papa dies, Lizzy will take over this house, and will lord it over us all."

Lydia's head ached as she chewed over the implications. No wonder Mama was so desperate for one of them to marry Mr. Collins! Mr. Collins may not have looked at plain old Mary, but Lydia had caught him glancing at her own bosom more than once. She was the handsomest of her sisters. She could capture Mr. Collins easily. She had not wanted to, but that was only because no one ever told her anything. And now it was too late. Lizzy had sunk her teeth into him, and in a few minutes, he would be hers.

Imagine being mistress of Longbourn! Lydia began to dream of the possibilities. She would have precedence over all her sisters, and they would need her permission if they wanted to buy a new hat or order a new gown. Why, even Mama would bow to her wishes! Lydia could plan dances and dinners with the officers. She would order a gleaming new carriage instead of that horrid old rattling coach that must be a hundred years old at least. And she would go to London, and promenade in Hyde Park to show off her fashionable clothes.

"Compose yourselves, girls," said Mrs. Bennet. "Mr. Collins will be here any moment to announce his engagement to Lizzy. It is very fortunate that Mr. Bennet was called away, for I can never know for certain how he will react and what he will say."

Lydia's dreams disappeared into thin air. The exciting new world slipped away, and she was left with miserable reality. *Lizzy* would have that life. *Lizzy* would have that control. *Lizzy* would lord it over them all and make them do what she wanted.

She hated Lizzy with a passion for taking her dreams from her.

"It is most unfair, Mama! Why did you not point him in my direction instead of hers?"

Kitty put down the hat she was trimming and stared at Lydia, dumbfounded.

"You! Marry Mr. Collins?" she said, laughing. "When you could have a handsome officer like Mr. Wickham? You have gone mad! Mr. Collins does not even know how to dance. Did you see how he stepped on Lizzy's feet yesterday at Netherfield and tore the lace trimming on her gown? You cannot stand being in the same room with him. You have told me so."

"That was before I realized that Lizzy would be mistress of Longbourn. Imagine having us all at her beck and call!" She looked at Mrs. Bennet. "Mama! How could you? You know she will spend all our money on stupid books for the library, instead of buying us new clothes. She will make us all miserable."

It was clear that Mrs. Bennett had not thought of it that way. Her eyes widened and she took out her lace handkerchief and began to fan herself.

"But Lydia, my dear, if I had known that you would wish it—if only—what a triumph it would have been – oh, Lydia. If I had thought for a moment that you were willing—"

"*I* would have married Mr. Collins," said Mary. "*I* was willing."

"Oh, hush, Mary," said Kitty. "You know he would never have married you. He was looking for a *pretty* wife."

Mary turned a most unbecoming shade of scarlet, put her book down and walked out of the room. Lydia rolled her eyes. After all, Kitty hadn't said anything that wasn't true. Mary had to know it would have been quite useless to set her cap at Mr. Collins. He would never look at her twice. Poor old Mary.

Now, if Lydia tried to win his affection...

"That was unkind, Kitty," said Jane. "And, Lydia, before you get carried away, remember that you would be *married* to Mr. Collins. All the money would be *his. He* would decide what to do with the money."

As if that mattered! Lydia knew she could wrap him around her little finger.

"La! Do you think I will not be able to manage

him? I am willing to wager that he will do whatever I ask."

"Lydia! You have been spending too much time with the officers," said Jane, gently. "Young ladies do not lay wagers."

As if Lydia cared for Jane's stuffy ideas. She had other things to worry about. She was crushed. All her hopes and dreams were dashed to the ground. Lizzy would have it all.

"It is so unfair, Mama!"

"I know, child, but it is too late," cried Mrs. Bennet. "If only we thought of it earlier. What a triumph it would have been for you!"

A huge sense of injustice filled Lydia. She would not let Lizzy take what was hers by right. She would not give up that easily.

An idea flashed into her mind. "You could interrupt," said Lydia. "You could stop Mr. Collins. It *isn't* too late, Mama. Please. You must."

A shrewd look passed through Mama's face, and hope leapt up in Lydia's heart.

"Hurry, Mama."

Mrs. Bennet rose swiftly to her feet. "Yes, yes, but I must have a reason. Come Lydia. *Hurry!* I will pretend to faint, and you will have to carry me."

"Carry you?" said Lydia doubtfully. Mama must be twice her weight at least. "But –"

"Do you want to marry Mr. Collins or not? Just do what I tell you. Now hurry, before it is too late.

When I faint, you must ask Mr. Collins to summon the apothecary, and tell him I have trouble breathing. Will you remember to say that?"

"Yes, of course Mama," said Lydia, running to the parlor behind Mama, her thoughts full of excitement. She would be mistress of Longbourn.

But first she must draw Mr. Collins' attention in some way. She looked down at the fichu that was supposed to preserve the modesty of her morning dress. Making sure no one noticed, she tore it away and threw it on the ground behind her. She pinched her cheeks and lips to make them more red. She wished she could stop in to look in a mirror to check her hair, but there was no time. Maybe if she let a few of her curls down. One of the officers—probably Mr. Chamberlayne—had told her that a loose curl on the side of her neck drove him to distraction.

By then they had reached the parlor, and there was no time to do anything else. Mama nodded quickly at Lydia and pushed the door open with a cry. The door hit the wall behind it with a loud crack, and Mama put her hand to her chest.

Mr. Collins was kneeling on one knee in front of Elizabeth.

"—the violence of my affections," he was saying.

What was this? Did Mr. Collins actually care for Elizabeth? No, it could not be. Lydia would be mistress of Longbourn.

"Help me!" cried Mama. "I cannot breathe."

She promptly put her hand to her chest and began to fall backwards. Lydia staggered under the full impact of Mama's weight as she crumpled, but managed to lower her—with great difficulty—to the ground.

"Oh, Mr. Collins!! You must summon the physician at once," said Lydia, acting her role with conviction because it would tear Mr. Collins away from Lizzy.

"But I have not finished my speech," he whined. "I—"

Mr. Collins was still kneeling and looking discomposed at having his speech interrupted. He simply stared, eyes bulging. He looked so ridiculous Lydia started to giggle, but she managed to hold it back just in time. And now Lizzy was running over to Mama and kneeling next to her. She would find out Mama was pretending, and she was such a pudding head, she would ruin everything. Lydia had to stop her.

"Mr. Collins, you must fetch the apothecary at once! Mama is taken ill!" What had Mama asked her to say? A heart problem? Breathing? No, that did not sound serious enough. She needed something that sounded truly alarming to get that lump Mr. Collins to do something.

Apoplexy. She didn't know what it was, but apoplexy was very serious. People always spoke about it in hushed tones.

She felt proud of herself for thinking of it.

"Apoplexy! Oh, you must hurry, sir."

"Surely not?" said Elizabeth. "But look, she is moving—oof!"

A kick in the back was enough to stop her silly sister from spoiling everything.

Mr. Collins' eyes widened at Elizabeth's exclamation. He finally staggered to his feet.

He was still looking dazed. Really, was the man completely useless? When she married him, she would have to take him in hand.

She made little shooing gestures at him as Elizabeth continued to feel Mama's pulse, her head lowered.

"Quickly, Mr. Collins," said Lydia, bursting into loud sobs. "You must fetch a doctor, before her heart gives way. And to think it has happened when there is no man in the house. We have only you. Papa is away. Oh, what shall we do? We are quite helpless."

"Fear not, Cousin," said Mr. Collins, clasping her hand and giving it a squeeze. She used the opportunity to swing her ringlets in his direction, so that they brushed against his face, and she bent over to allow him a view of what Mr. Carter had called her prized possessions. She felt a flush of triumph when Mr. Collins' eyes slid in that direction, then slid away.

She felt a glow of triumph. "I will make sure she will receive the best care. Have no fear, Cousin Lydia! You will not suffer a lack of male protection."

Mr. Collin beamed. It was entirely inappropriate under the circumstances, but Lydia was thrilled. She was making excellent progress.

"I knew I could count on you, Mr. Collins," she said, with a grateful smile. "Now you must fetch the apothecary at once, sir. Hurry!"

"But a servant—"

"The servants cannot be spared; besides, no one listens to them. Please?"

"Of course," said Mr. Collins, "I will go post-haste."

At this point Mama started to groan loudly. Lydia gave Mr. Collins a push and ushered him out of the door, then rushed to the window. She watched as Mr. Collins gave orders to have a horse saddled, then, as he rode away, she turned to Mama.

"You can stop now, Mama," said Lydia. "He is gone."

Mrs. Bennet stopped groaning and sat up.

"Thank goodness! I thought he would never leave!"

∞ ∞ ∞

Elizabeth dropped Mrs. Bennet's hand and sprang to her feet. She had no idea what game Mama and Lydia were playing, but she resented being part of it.

"What is the meaning of this?"

"La! Our ploy fooled even you, Lizzy!" said Lydia,

twirling around and laughing.

Elizabeth shook her head, vexed. As if she could possibly have been fooled, when Mama had actually winked at her!

"And next time, when we are in a situation like this, I would appreciate it if you would not kick me in the back. It *hurt*."

"I had to," said Lydia. "You are so silly, you might have given us away. How else could I warn you?"

There was no point having a sensible conversation with Lydia. Elizabeth sank into a chair as Kitty and Jane rushed into the room, with Mary following slowly behind.

"I saw Mr. Collins hurrying in the direction of the stables. Did it work?" cried Kitty.

"Yes!" Lydia took hold of Kitty's hands and the two began to caper around the room, giggling loudly.

"Will someone please enlighten me what all this is about?" said Elizabeth. "Why in heaven's name did Mama have to pretend to suffer an apoplexy?"

"It was the only way to prevent your marriage."

Elizabeth could only shake her head in bewilderment.

"But I thought you *wanted* me to marry Mr. Collins."

"I did not!" said Mrs. Bennet, hotly. "I never wanted any such thing."

"Really, Mama. It was you who prodded me into

the room and shut the door. I am certain if someone were to look closely, they would see bruises on my shoulders where you were poking me."

"Yes, well, that was before I knew Lydia wanted to marry him. She would make Mr. Collins a far more suitable wife than you would."

Elizabeth had never heard anything more preposterous. Lydia? A more suitable wife for Mr. Collins?

"Are you going to explain exactly what is going on?"

Mrs. Bennet and Lydia exchanged glances and fell into a stubborn silence. Elizabeth quirked her brow.

"If you do not tell me exactly what is happening, I will say the wrong things to Mr. Collins and spoil your plans. Besides, when all this is sorted, I am certain he will resume his proposal."

"Very well," said Mrs. Bennet, with a huff. "If you must know, it was the only way we could interrupt the proposal. It is only fair that Lydia should have a chance at Mr. Collins, don't you?"

"I would like a chance at Mr. Collins as well," interjected Mary.

"Hush, Mary!" said Mrs. Bennet.

Elizabeth stared at them in consternation. "Mama, what are you going to do when Mr. Crompton arrives? He will know at once that you are in perfect health."

"You need not concern yourself with the matter, Lizzy. You are a sly thing. You want me to recover at once, and say it was all a fuss about nothing, so that Mr. Collins will continue with his proposal, and you can steal him from Lydia. Your motives are very clear to me."

"You are completely mistaken, Mama. Lydia is more than welcome to Mr. Collins. I have no intention of marrying him. I was planning to reject his proposal."

"I am not such a fool, Lizzy, as to believe you would do something so ridiculous! Reject Mr. Collins, indeed, when he is the only one standing between us and destitution!"

Elizabeth saw it was impossible to convince Mama of the truth. Now that Lydia had set her mind on Mr. Collins, it was firmly entrenched in Mama's mind that Elizabeth would do everything to prevent the prospect.

"You may think as you chose, Mama, but I am telling you the truth. In any case, that is beside the point. Any moment now, Mr. Crompton will appear, and Jane and I will be expected to come up with some story to explain how you became ill."

Mrs. Bennet waved her objections away. "Leave that to me. I am quite capable of dealing with the apothecary. He has known me for years. Now go away and let me manage it."

"But Mama," objected Jane, weakly.

"You, too, Jane. I do not see why the two of you

are in such a dither. I thought you were supposed to be the sensible ones, but you are quite useless. Where has Lydia gone? Lydia will know how to behave."

Since when had Lydia been the model of practicality? It was truly astonishing how blind Mama was to her youngest daughter's faults. Elizabeth shook her head and took hold of Jane's hand.

"Come, Jane, let us leave Mama to it. We are clearly in the way."

A few minutes, later, they heard the bell ring, and she heard Mr. Crompton's voice.

Elizabeth sighed deeply.

"I am not happy about any of this," she said. "I only hope no one comes to hear of it. I wish Papa were here to put an end to all this nonsense. Why does this have to happen just when Papa is away? He never goes anywhere."

"Papa will be pleased to know that you already miss him when he has barely been gone half a day," said Jane, with a gentle smile, "But think of it this way. At least no one will pressure you into marrying Mr. Collins, so you have nothing to worry about."

Elizabeth could not help smiling. "You always try to find the good in every situation, Jane. In this instance, you are quite right."

She thought of Mr. Collins' blundering proposal and shuddered. "I shall be glad to be spared the problem of having to refuse him. You have no idea how awkward it was. I think it unfair that ladies are expected to sit through proposals and are expected to listen politely even when the gentleman's very manner of proposing is insulting." She took a deep breath. "I sincerely hope I will never have to listen to such a proposal again."

She shook her head. "I do not regret the interruption, but Mama is taking a risk by claiming to be very ill. What if someone were to hear of it?"

"No one will hear of it," said Jane reassuringly. "Mr. Crompton is discreet, and he is used to Mama's nervous ailments. The only person we need to worry about is Mr. Collins, and I am sure Mama knows how to deal with him. You can relax now in the knowledge that Mr. Collins is no longer your problem."

"You are right," said Elizabeth, throwing herself down on the bed with a smile. "The situation is completely in hand, and I cannot tell you how relieved I am."

Chapter 3

The apothecary, Mr. Crompton, arrived soon after. Elizabeth was impressed with the speed with which Mr. Collins was able to find him. It seemed she had misjudged her cousin.

Lydia came bouncing into the room a few minutes after he had climbed up to Mrs. Bennet's room.

"Kitty and I hate the sight of blood," she said. "You must go, Lizzy."

So much for leaving it to Mama to deal with the apothecary.

When she went into Mama's bedchamber, she found Mrs. Bennet pretending that she was too weak to move. Her left arm was hanging limply over the side of the bed.

Mr. Crompton was frowning as he prodded her

here and there, took her pulse, then asked for a bowl so he could blood-let her.

Mrs. Bennet gave a little moan, and Elizabeth knew she needed to put a stop to the bloodletting or Mama would faint in earnest.

"Do you believe bloodletting to be strictly necessary, Mr. Crompton? What have you discovered about her condition?"

He gestured for her to leave the room, he stepped aside to let her pass.

Knowing that Mama was perfectly healthy, she wondered what he would have to say. In a way, it was a test of his skill as a physician.

"To be perfectly honest, I am at a loss to diagnose her condition, Miss Elizabeth. Miss Lydia's description of what happened was rather vague and I have little to go by. Did you happen to witness what occurred?"

She shook her head. "It all happened so suddenly; I hardly know what to say."

Once again, she felt vexed at having to cover for her mother, but there was nothing else she could do.

"Quite understandable," he said, kindly. "With so little to go on, I cannot come up with anything definitive yet. I do not believe it is apoplexy, but it is difficult to tell in these situations. Her pulse is actually very strong – perhaps too strong— and indicates agitation rather than lethargy. In such situations, when there is an imbalance in the humors, bloodletting can be a way to overcome that imbalance."

"But is it really necessary?"

"I will be forthright with you, Miss Elizabeth. In cases such as apoplexy, very little can be done for the patient. They might recover, or they might not. At this stage, I do not see any definite signs of apoplexy. We will have to wait and see if it progresses. For now, apart from draining the blood, all I can do is prescribe her some laudanum, and let nature take its course."

"If you are not entirely sure, can we postpone the bloodletting, Mr. Crompton?"

Mr. Crompton was not happy with the suggestion, but after returning to the bedroom and checking her pulse once again, he gave a quick nod.

"Very well. But you must promise that if her condition changes in any way, you will send for me at once."

He produced a bottle of tincture and provided Elizabeth with instructions about when and how to give it to her. Then, with a quick bow, he took his leave.

As soon as the front door had opened and closed, and the clip clop of the horseshoes against the cobbles indicated that Mr. Crompton was riding away, Mrs. Bennet sat up.

"We cannot keep up this pretense, Mama, it is not fair to Mr. Crompton. He is very puzzled."

"I do not see how it is unfair, Elizabeth. I am sure your papa will compensate him handsomely."

"But Mama—"

She did not continue. It was clear Mrs. Bennet had lost interest and was not paying her the least attention.

Elizabeth sighed. It did not really matter, after all. She felt sorry that Mr. Crompton was so perplexed, but it was not a serious matter. Mama would be on her feet again soon, and it would all be behind them.

A few minutes later, Lydia hurried in to announce that Mr. Bingley and Mr. Darcy were riding up the drive.

"La!" said Lydia, "Why is it that Mr. Darcy always follows Mr. Bingley around? We can never have any peace."

She threw herself onto the bed next to Mama with a loud moan.

It occurred to Elizabeth that it was unusual for Mr. Darcy and Mr. Bingley to come calling at this time of day, especially after a ball that had ended in the early hours of the morning.

"More to the point," she said, "why are they here now?"

"Because Mr. Bingley cannot stay away from Jane, of course," said Mrs. Bennet. "Help me up. I must go down to see Mr. Bingley."

Elizabeth's sense of unease was growing.

"You cannot do that yet, Mama," she objected. "Suppose they ran into Mr. Crompton, and he told them you are ill? It would look very strange if you came downstairs, fit as a fiddle. You had better stay here, Mama. I will talk to them and let you know if you are free to come down."

She hurried to her room to prepare Jane to receive their visitors. Jane rushed to the mirror to check her reflection, but barely had time before the bell rang forcefully three times.

"That must be Mr. Darcy," said Jane, her eyes widening. "Mr. Bingley would not ring so loudly."

Mr. Darcy would not ring so loudly either, not unless he had heard the news. Elizabeth's heart sank. It was looking more and more likely that the news of Mama's illness had reached them.

"Will you receive our visitors, Jane? I must stop Mama from coming down."

Jane's eyes widened in horror. "Do you think they know?"

"I hope not, but we cannot take the risk."

Elizabeth hurried to Mama's bedchamber just as she tugged at the bellpull.

"Oh, where is Hill? I need her at once! We must invite Mr. Bingley for dinner—I must tell Cook--"

"Mama, Hill is answering the door. You must listen to me. You cannot go down. Think what will happen if Mr. Collins comes in to find you sitting with your guests."

Lydia jumped up. "Oh, that would be dreadful! Then he may propose to Lizzy again. We cannot allow that."

"Where is the dratted Mr. Collins anyway?" Mrs.

Bennet said peevishly.

Elizabeth mustered all the patience she had. It was Mama who had created this situation to start with, and now she was the one who had to deal with the consequences.

"You know very well that Mr. Collins went to the village to summon the apothecary. *You* wanted him to go, Mama. *You* sent him."

"Well, if he had returned as quickly as he should, we could have told him I was much improved," said Mrs. Bennet, "and we would have been finished with the whole thing."

"Then Lizzy would have married him." Lydia pouted. "And it would all have been for nothing."

There was an obvious way to resolve the whole debacle. "I have already told you. I have no intention of marrying Mr. Collins."

Lydia and Mama stared at Elizabeth as if she had sprouted horns, then decided she did not mean it. Choosing to ignore her, they went back to arguing.

"I mean it." Elizabeth said, louder this time.

The words fell on deaf ears. Mama was twisting her lace handkerchief around her thumb – a sign that she was about to have an attack of the nerves – and Lydia was chewing her nails.

By now Elizabeth was growing very anxious, conscious of the two gentlemen who had been admitted into the parlor downstairs, and worried that Mama's voice would carry.

In the end, it was Lydia who clinched the matter. "If you go downstairs, Mama, I will never talk to you again!"

She burst into tears.

That was enough to convince Mama, who plumped up her pillows irritably and settled back into her bed, prepared to be fussed over.

"Very well, then, I will stay here. But you must have Cook make my favorite jam tarts. Oh, and tell her I would like some Mulligatawny soup. It is a pity that Mr. Bennet is away and cannot bring me rabbit. I do think it will improve my health."

To Elizabeth's intense relief, by the time Mrs. Hill came up to announce the gentlemen's arrival, Mrs. Bennet had half-convinced herself she was an invalid and needed to be cossetted. Elizabeth left the room and shut the door, only to find Jane hovering outside, too shy to go downstairs alone.

Elizabeth pulled at Jane's sleeve, and together they descended the stairs.

And so, with her conscience snapping at her heels, Elizabeth descended to face the consequences, crossing her fingers that Mr. Darcy and Mr. Bingley knew nothing.

Darcy did not like Mrs. Bennet, and he had the

feeling it was mutual. Nevertheless, he could not forget that Mrs. Bennet was Elizabeth's mother. Having himself lost a mother at a tender age, he knew the pain and sorrow that accompanied such a situation. He did not hold out much hope that Mrs. Bennet would recover. Apoplexy was almost always fatal, and if it was not, the consequences were severe. Some victims lost their physical functions, others their speech. He had even heard of family members who were placed in asylums because their relatives believed they had gone mad.

It was difficult to imagine Mrs. Bennet stripped of her ability to speak, considering how loud her voice usually was. The possibility that her speech might be affected saddened him, somehow, even if he had disliked her shrill way of talking.

The housekeeper had asked them to sit down, but Darcy was too worried to do anything but pace up and down the small parlor. As soon as Elizabeth and Miss Bennet entered the room, he hastened over to them. Once he reached them, however, he realized he did not know quite what to do.

Seeking refuge in civility, he took up Elizabeth's hand and bowed. Then, because she looked at him with such confusion, he was overcome with a wave of tenderness. His heart ached for her. Unable to hold back, he covered her hand with his and pressed her fingers gently, hoping to reassure her.

"We came as soon as we were able," he said. "I hope the apothecary has good news."

She winced and looked distressed. He longed to take her into his arms and hold her close.

"Mama is doing well, sir. The apothecary is inclined to think she will recover soon."

No doubt the apothecary had tried to spare her the worst.

"Yes," he said. "Yes. We must always hope for the best."

Elizabeth turned her face away, avoiding his gaze, hiding her tears. She was always so strong, perhaps she considered them a sign of weakness.

Where was his presence of mind? The least he could do was offer her his handkerchief. He noticed with mortification that he was still holding her hand. He pressed it once again, let go, and reached for his pocket.

"Miss Elizabeth."

She stared at the handkerchief in bewilderment.

"No, no, sir. I do not need it." She stepped away from it as if he had just offered her poison.

He put the offending article away, feeling snubbed.

"I understand that these are very difficult circumstances. We are here to offer our—support."

He flushed at how close he had come to saying the wrong thing. He had been thinking of 'condolences'.

Elizabeth took a deep breath. "You are mistaken, sir—"

To his surprise, her sister Jane interrupted her. "Thank you, Mr. Darcy. And Mr. Bingley. How kind of you to come to our assistance."

Her voice was firm – firmer than he had ever heard it. There was a warning there, too.

He looked from one to the other, trying to work out what was happening. Then it occurred to him that Elizabeth was reluctant to accept his help. After all, he was a single young gentleman, and it was only too easy for such assistance to be misconstrued.

Very probably, Elizabeth meant to send him and Mr. Bingley on their way. She thought they were intruding. It was completely understandable, of course. She was distressed, and she needed time to sort herself out.

Nevertheless, it hurt.

Chapter 4

E lizabeth scarcely knew where to look. There was no doubting the sincerity in Mr. Darcy's expression. At that moment, she was certain he would go to any length to help her. A crushing weight of guilt settled over her. She could not allow him to continue in his belief that Mama had been struck down by such a terrible condition. Besides, the longer they continued to dissemble, the more entangled the situation would become.

All her instincts drove her to tell the truth. She could not allow the two gentlemen to exhibit so much concern, knowing full well that Mama, far from being ill, was at present upstairs in perfect health, plotting how to secure Longbourn for Lydia, and feasting on her favorite foods.

But Jane had another view of the matter. She was glaring at Elizabeth, her expression clearly conveying that she would not allow it. Jane – who rarely opposed anyone – had intervened and prevented her from confessing.

It was so rare for Jane to be forceful, Elizabeth wavered. The need to tell the truth was becoming a compulsion, but if Mr. Bingley took offence and left Netherfield, if he did not ask for Jane's hand, Elizabeth would never forgive herself, and to judge by her warning, Jane would never forgive her either.

She turned her back and walked to the window as she struggled to master her feelings, which were pulling her in two directions at once.

Then the doorbell jingled, and Mr. Collins hurried into the room. The decision was taken from her. Saying anything at this point would not only affect Jane's chances, but Lydia's as well.

The truth would have to wait.

"A thousand apologies." Mr. Collins was huffing and puffing as if he had been running all the way from Meryton. "I am not familiar with the neighborhood. I could not find my way back and had to request assistance several times. Has the apothecary examined Mrs. Bennet?"

Jane would have to answer that one. Elizabeth was fast becoming tired of this question. If Jane did not want her to reveal the truth, she would have to be prepared to dissemble. Elizabeth was not such an accomplished actress that she would go so far as to pretend an anxiety over her mother she did not feel. Jane was always better at concealing her feelings.

Meanwhile, Mr. Darcy's gaze was fixed on her in such a compassionate, warm way, Elizabeth could not help feeling flattered. He had always looked at her to find fault. For the first time, she was seeing a different side of him. Under any other circumstances, she might even have found it thrilling.

"Thank you for your concern, sir," Jane was saying. "Mr. Crompton has been to see her, and he has given her a drought."

It was all true, though it side-stepped the main point. Jane was quite good at this. Her color was heightened, but otherwise, she looked as serene as ever.

Mr. Collins took up her words immediately.

"All thanks to Mr. Darcy. If it were not for his speedy actions, she may not have survived the worst. You can be sure that I will inform my patroness, Lady Catherine--"

"—You exaggerate, sir," said Mr. Darcy, interrupting what everyone knew would be a diversion into praising Lady Catherine. "I did nothing more than my duty. I was glad to be of service to Miss Elizabeth – and her sisters."

He was looking intently at Elizabeth. Had she imagined the hesitation?

Why was he suddenly paying her such particular attention? She felt flustered and hot. She was not accustomed to being the object of Mr. Darcy's interest.

Now she was being absurd. Mr. Darcy wanted to offer his support, nothing more.

"I will send for my physician to come down from London," said Mr. Bingley, talking to Jane, wishing to receive some credit in the role of hero.

"I assure you, sir, it is entirely unnecessary," said Elizabeth, wishing they could talk of something else. "We would be grateful to accept your very generous offer, if it were needed. But it is not. I thank you for your kindness. The apothecary has assured us that it is not serious."

Mr. Darcy gave her an approving look.

"You are being very brave, Miss Elizabeth."

"Not at all," she said, starting to grow vexed. "I am entirely serious when I say I do not think Mama's condition is dire."

"Be it as it may be, it is too much to deal with when Mr. Bennet is not here. If you give me your father's direction, I will send an express to him at once."

Heavens! This was really going too far! Now Papa would be obliged to abandon his friend and return to Longbourn.

"Thank you, Mr. Darcy, but there is no need. Mama is resting and should improve in a day or two. Papa is visiting a friend of his from Oxford who is gravely ill. I would not like to call him back unless it was strictly necessary."

"Miss Elizabeth does have a point, Darcy," interjected Bingley. "Perhaps we ought to wait. No need to cause unnecessary anxiety, you know."

Darcy looked grim. "If I were Mr. Bennet, I would certainly want to know what was happening in my own home."

Papa would *not* want to know what a muddle Mama had created.

"I would rather wait before sending for him," said Elizabeth, irritated by Mr. Darcy's persistence.

"We cannot keep such a serious matter from him, surely," said Mr. Darcy. "What if Mrs. Bennet's condition takes a turn for the worse? How long would it take him to come back? How far away is his friend?"

"It is a two days' journey," said Jane. "He is staying with Lord Beauford, in Gloucestershire."

"Then it would be wise to send for him."

"If you do not mind, Mr. Darcy, I think *we* should make the decision. I promise you that if Mama's condition grows worse, I will send a note to Netherfield, and then you can do what you believe is best," said Elizabeth, wondering how on earth she could extricate herself from such a coil.

"Cousin Elizabeth," Mr. Collins interfered with an obsequious smile. "In the absence of a male guardian at a time of crisis like this, it behooves me to take charge in a household of delicate females. Do not concern yourself with such matters. I will discuss the issue with Mr. Darcy, and we will reach a conclusion together."

Elizabeth did not miss the contemptuous look Darcy sent him. Serve him right if he ended up cloistered in the library with Mr. Collins. At this point, she just wished them all gone.

She bit back the angry retort she wanted to fling at her cousin. While she cared nothing for the opinions of Mr. Collins and Mr. Darcy, she did not wish to offend Mr. Bingley.

Rational thought intervened. There was no escaping the fact that, if Mama's illness had been real, Elizabeth would have sent for Papa immediately. How could she possibly justify keeping her father in the dark about something like this?

"It might be for the best, Miss Elizabeth," said Bingley, with a gentle smile.

"Very well," she said, with a sigh. "But you must allow me a few minutes to pen Papa a quick note."

"Of course, Cousin Elizabeth," said Mr. Collins. "Take as much time as you need. My experience with my flock has shown me that painful matters like this require patience and clarity of thought. If you wish me to advise you on the best phrasing to use on such an occasion, I would be more than happy to do so."

"Thank you, Cousin, but I am quite capable of writing a note to Papa by myself."

Elizabeth went to the escritoire in the corner of the parlor and wrote a quick note to Mr. Bennet. Knowing that Mr. Collins was likely to look over her shoulder while she wrote, she tried to word the letter in a way her father would understand without being told.

Dear Papa,
Do not be alarmed when you receive this note. Mama has had an attack. Mr. Crompton has been to see her, and we hope she will be up and about in a few days. I will send an express if there is any need for you to come.
Yours, Lizzy

From the corner of her eye, she saw Mr. Collins stand up and head in her direction. There was no time to think further about the wording. She folded it and took out a wafer from the box. Licking the wafer quickly, she managed to slip it under the fold just as Mr. Collins reached her and put out his hand for the letter.

"I would like to add a few compassionate words if I may, Cousin Elizabeth. It is important to assure Mr. Bennet that all the young ladies of the household are in my good hands and will want for nothing. With the distinguished Mr. Darcy's assistance, and my endless compassion for my cousins in this dark hour, you will be well taken care of. I am certain he will be relieved to hear it."

"It will not be necessary sir," she said, with a smile, taking up the seal. "I am certain you would prefer to take your time to find the exact wording, and this is a very hurried note. Surely you do not wish to outshine me, sir."

Mr. Collins smiled condescendingly. "Your modesty does you credit. Naturally, I do not expect a lady to have the facility in writing that a clergyman has, so you need not be embarrassed. I have studied the Classical Languages and the works of the ancient masters. I am more than proficient in my writing. In fact, my great patroness, Lady Catherine--"

Elizabeth threw a quick glance towards Mr. Darcy. She expected to see him looking severe, but he was watching her with a small smile playing on his lips. His dark eyes were soft. When he was not looking down his nose at everyone, she realized, he was very handsome. Attractive, even, with his broad shoulders and the tumble of fashionable dark curls spread across his brow.

Darcy's lips twitched. Had he guessed the direction of her thinking? She looked away quickly, heat flooding into her face.

She managed to seal the letter just as Mr. Collins took it from her hand. The pattern was lopsided, but at least Mr. Collins would not go so far as to unseal it and read what she had written.

"It is too late, Mr. Collins. However, you are welcome to send Papa an express telling him your sentiments when we have more news."

There was a cough from the corner of the room where Mr. Darcy was sitting. Was he laughing at her? When she looked at him directly, however, she found his eyes fixed on her face with a curious expression. His look was so piercing, she squirmed.

Then he stood up and came in her direction.

"Miss Elizabeth, I wonder if I might have a word with you concerning your mother."

"Certainly," she replied, her heart starting to hammer. Had Mr. Darcy guessed the truth?

"If you would be kind enough to step into the hallway?"

Mr. Collins looked like he might join them, but Mr. Darcy quelled him with a glance, and he slunk back and returned to the seat he had occupied earlier.

"After you, Miss Elizabeth."

Darcy waited politely for her to proceed him out of the door. He sounded so stern, Elizabeth knew the game was up.

She passed by him, feeling self-conscious and miserable.

Not wanting to face him alone, she sent a look of entreaty to Jane, but her sister was engaged with Mr. Bingley and did not even look in Elizabeth's direction.

She prepared herself for the worst. She would rise to the occasion. She would not be intimidated.

Mr. Collins was watching them with hawk eyes as they left the parlor. Elizabeth turned her back to him so he would not witness her humiliation and prepared to deal with whatever blow she was about to receive.

"I know these situations can be awkward, and you may not be willing to receive assistance from someone you have not known for very long. I understand that pride can sometimes get in the way."

This was not what she had expected.

"Of course. I hope I do not seem ungrateful, sir."

"I am not saying this because I expect gratitude," he replied. "I just want to assure you that you need not feel alone. I am at your disposal, Miss Elizabeth, any time, night or day."

His voice was warm and deep and completely unfamiliar. She stood frozen in place, not quite sure how to respond to this unexpected side of him. Was this the same Mr. Darcy who had snubbed her at the Meryton Assembly? It seemed impossible.

She would have liked to laugh dismissively, but the intensity of his gaze did not allow it. She shifted uneasily and looked away, her conscience gnawing at her, nagging her to tell the truth.

If only she could put an end to the charade.

"Would you ring for refreshments, Lizzy? You are close to the bellpull."

It was yet another reminder from Jane, who must have sensed that Elizabeth was weakening again.

Elizabeth gave Darcy a regretful smile. "I will not forget your offer, sir, nor your kindness."

She did not wait for his response. She could not look him fully in the face again. Instead, she escaped to the parlor to join the others.

It was a coward's way out, but there was nothing she could do about it.

As Mrs. Hill brought in pies and cold meats several minutes later, Lydia sauntered into the room and sat next to Mr. Collins.

"May I help you to some steak and ale pie, Mr. Collins?" said Lydia, very sweetly.

Then, handing him his plate, she added, "I wanted to thank you for your speedy actions this morning. It is thanks to you that Mama is on the road to recovery."

Mr. Collins' eyes darted towards Mr. Darcy, but Lydia was smiling so tenderly at him, he could not bring himself to give credit to someone else.

"It was nothing," he said. "I merely did my duty, something I always aspire to do. In fact, her ladyship —"

He was about to embark on yet another long monologue extolling his own virtues along with Lady Catherine's. Mr. Darcy's mouth was curling in distaste.

Elizabeth groaned inwardly and turned to Mr. Bingley to deflect everyone's attention from Mr. Collins.

"Miss Bingley must be pleased the ball was so successful. It was indeed a very enjoyable evening."

"It certainly was, Miss Elizabeth," said Mr. Bingley. "My sister is experienced in organizing balls. There is nothing she does not know about them. She always ensures that everything runs smoothly, and that everyone is in good spirits." He sent Jane a significant glance. "I especially enjoyed the musicians. It was a good orchestra, was it not, Miss Bennet? My sister arranged for them to come down from London."

Jane blushed as she found herself the center of attention.

"It is one of the best I have been privileged to hear."

Bingley beamed widely.

Elizabeth flicked a quick glance towards Mr. Darcy. He had gone back to looking severe and silent as usual. She felt disappointed. It was as if that little interlude in the hallway had never happened.

"Perhaps we can have another ball soon," said Mr. Bingley.

Mr. Darcy scowled.

"Oh, yes!" said Lydia. "But you must have it soon, before Mr. Collins leaves, or he will miss it."

"Are you planning to leave us, then, Mr. Collins?" said Mr. Bingley, amiably.

"I am needed by my honorable patroness," said Mr. Collins. "And by my flock, of course. I was hoping to return in time for the Sunday service in four days, but events have intervened."

"Surely there is no hurry, Mr. Collins?" said Lydia, all smiles. "You must stay longer. You can ask the curate to deliver the sermon. That is what they are for. I am sure Lady Constance can spare you."

Mr. Collins' expression fluctuated between a grimace and a smile. "Lady *Catherine* de Bourgh was kind enough to permit me time to pay my respects to my cousins, and to offer an olive branch, but I do not wish to provoke her wrath by staying away too long."

"I can safely speak on behalf of my aunt," said Mr. Darcy, abruptly, "As long as there is a curate in place, I do not suppose you will be missed."

He stood up. "And now, I need to take my leave. If we may, we will call on you again tomorrow to ensure all is well."

He bowed stiffly and turned to his friend.

"Bingley, are you coming?"

Bingley stood up, looking sheepish. "Yes, of course. I hope we have not overstayed our welcome."

He bowed quickly and followed Darcy, who was already striding out of the room.

Chapter 5

Darcy awoke the next morning in a state of anxiety. Elizabeth had been dismissive, but what if the apothecary was wrong? What if something had happened during the night?

He did not like sitting around twiddling his thumbs when Elizabeth could be in intense distress. Even waiting for Evans to shave him had him squirming with impatience.

When he did finally make it downstairs, he found Bingley already in the breakfast room, chewing desolately on a piece of buttered toast.

"I was thinking of riding to Longbourn," he said, by way of greeting.

Bingley looked shocked. "We cannot call on them at eight o'clock in the morning."

They both looked at the clock on the mantlepiece, where the time was a few minutes past eight.

The irony did not escape Darcy. That Bingley should be urging control showed how far-gone Darcy was.

"Though I must admit I have been thinking the same thing myself this past half-hour." Bingley sighed. "If only society did not have quite so many rules!"

"Without those rules," said Darcy blandly, "we would be little more than savages."

Bingley sighed, his gaze flicking once again to the clock. "I suppose so."

"It is no use staring at the clock. You know what they say. A watched kettle never boils," said Darcy.

Bingley gave a lopsided grin. "I have never had the privilege of watching a kettle boil."

"Neither have I," said Darcy.

The two gentlemen fell into silence. Just for something to do, Darcy went to the side-table and helped himself. He was not in the least hungry, and he did not care what he ate.

"I thought you disliked kippers," remarked Bingley, when Darcy came back to the table.

Darcy looked down at his plate. He had indeed served himself a pile of kippers.

"Well spotted, Bingley. Clearly I was too pre-occupied."

He pushed the kippers to the side of the plate and picked up the buttered toast. He did not know what the day would bring, and it would be good to be fortified, just in case.

The food turned to sawdust on his tongue. He tossed down the rest of the toast in disgust.

"I have been meaning to talk to you, Bingley. What the devil did you mean yesterday by offering to have another ball?"

Bingley looked shamefaced. "I was carried away, Darcy. I felt that it would be a good distraction, under the circumstances, something for everyone to look forward to."

"And how do you imagine Miss Bennet will feel when you do not follow up on your promise because you have left for London?"

"It was not a promise, Darcy, just a possibility."

Darcy shook his head, but today he was more understanding of Bingley's impulse. Darcy would have done anything if he could help Elizabeth feel better, but he was not the kind of person that sugar-coated anything. He could never promise anything he could not fulfill, as Bingley had done. It seemed too much like a lie, and he had a horror of lies. Disguise of every sort was his abhorrence.

Still, strictly speaking, Bingley was not lying, and he meant no harm.

"Do you think Mrs. Bennet is likely to improve?"

It was a question Darcy had asked himself multiple times.

"I have no idea. I have not seen her, so I cannot make any judgement." He could only hope that nothing worse had happened since yesterday.

The two gentlemen fell into silence, contemplating the possibilities. For several minutes, the only sound in the room was the clink of silverware against China, interspersed with the sound of coffee being sipped, and the monotonous ticking of the clock.

Darcy's mind drifted to Elizabeth and the way she had looked when he was there. She was always so pert, so sure of herself, always with a ready answer on those bold lips. It shook him to find her so agitated and distracted. In normal circumstances, she always met his gaze directly, her fine eyes vivacious, bright with laughter or defiance. Yesterday her expression had been restrained, as if she had drawn a curtain to conceal her feelings.

The image of Elizabeth sitting anxiously at her mother's bedside was imprinted on his mind. Darcy wished he could be there, holding her hand and consoling her, but it was not in his power to do so.

"If only we could do something," said Bingley.

It occurred to Darcy that there *was* something he could do.

Elizabeth had refused to have her father's trip interrupted, but she needed support, and that fool Collins was worse than useless; he was a liability.

"I will send my carriage for Mr. Bennet."

"Are you sure? Miss Elizabeth was not enamored of that idea."

"Would you like it if someone kept a secret of this kind from you?"

Bingley gave it a moment's thought. "No. I suppose not."

"There you are, then. I shall go and give instructions."

Bingley nodded. "And then we will go to Longbourn. You never know. Something unexpected may have happened."

His presence would probably be superfluous, but he could not help remembering how subdued Elizabeth was yesterday. From there it was an easy step to convince himself that she might be in dire need of his assistance.

And besides, he really wanted to see her.

It was morning, and they were all assembled in the parlor. Mary was reading a sermon aloud, significantly entitled 'On the Sin of Lying'. There was no question Mary had chosen the topic deliberately. Elizabeth was wriggling in her seat, worrying that Lydia or Kitty would grow tired of Mary's preaching and blurt out something that would let the cat out of the bag. Lydia was already having a hard time controlling her laughter, and Kitty was giggling behind her kerchief.

Mr. Collins was smiling with approval at Mary,

interrupting every now and then to elaborate on some specific theological doctrine the author of the piece was referring to. Since Mr. Collins' explanations were sprinkled with an abundance of Greek phrases, the explanations hindered rather than assisted their understanding. Elizabeth suspected that Mr. Collins was more interested in showing off his grasp of Greek than he was in clarifying the text.

Elizabeth's thoughts drifted instead to Mr. Darcy.

She still did not know what to make of Mr. Darcy's behavior the day before. There was something in his eye she could not quite identify. If it was anyone else, she might have called it admiration.

Tolerable, but not handsome enough to tempt me. That was what he had said at the Meryton Assembly.

Mr. Darcy did not admire her, she said firmly to herself. He thought her barely tolerable. It would not do to read too much into it. He was a dutiful gentleman, and he was simply trying to be neighborly, believing their circumstances to be ominous.

Still, she could not deny that Mr. Darcy was a far better person than she had originally thought. She admired the way he had taken charge and done what was needed. Unlike Papa, who would diddle and dither when confronted with an emergency, Darcy acted quickly. He had stepped in and taken the Bennet ladies under his wing without a fuss, and without the slightest trace of the arrogant attitude Elizabeth had considered as his main characteristic. True, he had ignored Elizabeth's attempts to dissuade him from sending an express to Papa—there was some arrogance in that—but he meant well, and she could not fault that under the circumstances.

One only had to compare him to Mr. Bingley, who had behaved in a perfectly gentlemanly manner, but had not showed the same resolution and determination. Of the two, she felt, Mr. Darcy had come off as the better man. And, of course, he was head and shoulders superior to Mr. Collins, both metaphorically and literally.

The problem was, it was impossible to think of Mr. Darcy without being consumed by guilt. Why did he suddenly have to reveal another side of him just when she was engaged in a deception? Until now, Elizabeth had convinced herself—with her forthright character—of her own superiority over him, but she no longer had a leg to stand on. Darcy's gaze seemed to dig into her very soul, and she *cringed* at what he would find. Yet she had no idea how to get herself out of it. She could not expose Lydia to the mockery of strangers for having decided to secure Mr. Collins for herself. Nor could she make Mama the target of their disdain.

Feeling full of restless energy, she jumped to her feet suddenly, interrupting Mr. Collins in mid-sentence.

"I need to consult the apothecary," she said. "Jane and I will walk into Meryton."

Mr. Collins looked none too pleased at the interruption, but he recovered quickly.

"Of course, Cousin. It is quite to be expected that you are experiencing anxiety. We can all walk there together."

∞ ∞ ∞

As they set out on the walk, Lydia left nothing to chance. She made sure to take Mr. Collins' arm all the way to Meryton. Elizabeth was only too happy to have Mr. Collins' attention drawn elsewhere. She did not know what Lydia found to talk about if she was not talking of hats and officers, but one way or the other, she kept up a steady conversation.

When they reached the village, several of the officers bowed to them and greeted them, but Lydia ignored them completely. Elizabeth was both astonished and amused. Was Lydia seriously willing to give up flirting with the officers to become mistress of Longbourn?

Elizabeth remained skeptical. Still, as long as it prevented Mr. Collins from proposing, Elizabeth would be happy to provide Lydia with all the help in the world.

As they reached the village, Elizabeth and Jane excused themselves and slipped into the apothecary's. Elizabeth needed to have a clearer idea of what could be expected if someone had suffered an apoplexy, and there was no one else who could tell her, other than

Mr. Crompton.

The bell on the door tinkled as it opened, and Mr. Crompton came quickly through a back door, looking like an owl with his round eyes, round spectacles, and whisps of downy white hair. His expression changed when he saw them, and he came quickly around the counter to the front of the shop.

"Miss Bennet, Miss Elizabeth!" he said, forgetting even to bow. "Has Mrs. Bennet taken a turn for the worse?"

Once again, Elizabeth felt terrible that she had to continue with the farce.

"No, no, not at all," she said quickly. "She is in fact much improved. We simply wanted to ask you what to expect next. She is awake and eager to leave her bed. Is that normal? Is it safe for her to do so?"

"Did she suffer no other effects? No confusion in her speech? No weakness in her limbs?"

"Not at all, Mr. Crompton."

"Then she has had a most fortunate escape, and I am pleased to hear it," he said, relieved. "I would not advise her to rise from her bed quite yet. We would not wish to risk the possibility of a relapse. It is important for her to rest for a few days. I will call on her this evening."

"Thank you, Mr. Crompton," said Jane. "Your assistance is very much appreciated."

They curtsied and left the shop. Elizabeth slipped her arm into the crook of her sister's.

"I feel awful."

"I do, too, especially when I am with Mr. Bingley and Mr. Darcy," said Jane. "I am in constant fear that something will show on my face."

Elizabeth snorted. "That is hardly likely. Your expression reveals nothing at all." She paused. "Maybe we should tell them the truth."

Jane looked stricken. "You cannot be serious! What will Mr. Bingley think?"

"If he cares about you – and we both know that he does – you can both laugh at it and that will be the end of it."

"No, Lizzy," said Jane firmly. "I cannot risk it. I am not so certain of his affection as *that*."

It was a risk, of course. Elizabeth did not blame her for wanting to avoid it. Jane was not the type to take chances.

"It can be a kind of test, I suppose," Elizabeth speculated.

Jane shook her head vigorously. "A test? What makes you think I want to put Mr. Bingley's affection to the test, Lizzy? If he cares for me, he will reveal it in his own time." She gave a little smile. "It does not matter in any case. You heard Mr. Crompton. Mama will soon be up and about, and it will all be forgotten."

"Perhaps."

Elizabeth was not convinced, and she was still not happy about the situation. Her conscience was hurting, and she was worried, too, that Mr. Darcy would see through their pretense. After his kindness yesterday, she could not bear to deceive him.

"Very well, then," said Elizabeth, resigning to the inevitable. "I am becoming more proficient at lying by the hour. If I am not careful, it will become a habit, and my character will be forever changed."

"Nonsense, Lizzy! In any case, I do not see how we can put a stop to it. There is no way out of this tangle."

Even after they joined the others, Jane's comment occupied Elizabeth's mind all the way back to Longbourn.

∞ ∞ ∞

Far from being too early, Darcy and Bingley arrived just as the Bennets were returning from their walk. Mr. Darcy enquired anxiously about Mrs. Bennet, and Jane replied that she was already much improved.

Mr. Darcy's relief at this news was palpable. As he bowed, he took up Elizabeth's hand and held it, then gave her such a luminous smile that she felt completely dazzled. His hand burned into hers, even through their gloves, and she had to draw it away instantly, taken by surprise.

They all barely had time to be seated when the doorbell sounded, and the voice of Aunt Phillips could be heard asking if they had any visitors.

She bustled quickly into the room.

"Since my sister is indisposed, and Mr. Bennet away," said Mrs. Philips, with relish, "I have come to act as chaperone. One cannot be too careful about young ladies' reputations."

"Very true—" began Mary.

"Quite right, Mrs. Philips," said Mr. Collins, interrupting. "As a clergyman—"

Mrs. Philips ignored him.

"I expected you last night, Lydia and Kitty," said their aunt. "I can understand that Jane and Lizzy are needed to nurse their mama, but you could have gotten away. All the officers were asking after you."

Lizzy was mortified at Mrs. Philips' words. She threw a quick look at Mr. Darcy and saw his mouth tighten. The luminous smile was gone.

"Officers?" said Lydia. "La! What would I want with officers, when I have the company of far more worthy gentlemen?"

She looked at Mr. Collins as she spoke, and he inclined his head, his expression full of complacency.

Mrs. Philips stared.

"But only two days ago you said—"

It was time to intervene.

"If you have come to enquire about Mama's health, then I am pleased to say she is improving fast," said Elizabeth. She had promised herself that she would not utter any more falsehoods, but someone had to keep her aunt in check, and Jane was not doing it. "She is sitting up in bed today. We are hoping she will be on her feet in a few days."

"That is excellent news!" Mr. Bingley beamed. "You must be intensely relieved, Miss Bennet."

Jane blushed and looked at her hands.

"Yes, very much so," she murmured, shyly.

"Then I will go up and speak to your mama at once!"

Elizabeth was taken aback. She had not considered that possibility. If Aunt Philips went upstairs she would discover that Mama was perfectly well, and the news would be all over Meryton in an hour.

"Perhaps it would be better to wait another two or three days until we are sure she is ready to receive visitors."

"Nonsense! I am sure she would love to see me. I will entertain her with the latest gossip."

In a few minutes, everything would unravel. Mama would be bound to tell Aunt Philips the news, and the whole sorry debacle would be known.

"Mrs. Philips," said Darcy, abruptly. "We were thinking of going into Meryton. I would like to send some lace to my sister. The haberdasher has acquired a new sample, I have heard. I wonder if you can lend me your excellent judgement on the matter?"

Everyone stared including Mr. Bingley, whose mouth hung open for a full minute before he caught on and lent Darcy his assistance.

He gave her a charming smile. "It is an urgent matter, Mrs. Philips. Lace is not readily available in Derbyshire."

"Really?" said Mrs. Philips, looking very superior, her eyes darting towards Mr. Darcy. "Well, Meryton may be a small place, but no one can say we are backward."

Before anyone knew it, Mr. Darcy had taken Mrs. Philips by the elbow and was guiding her to the door. As he left the room, he sent Elizabeth a meaningful glance, and then he did the most shocking thing.

He winked at her.

Elizabeth looked around to see if anyone else had witnessed it, but no one was paying attention. Had he really winked? Laughter bubbled up inside her, along with an entirely new sensation of well-being.

She was only too aware of the sacrifice Mr. Darcy was making. He would be obliged to spend the next hour in the company of Aunt Philips, walking to Meryton, then looking at lace.

He would do this for them? Why? She thought of that strange light in his eyes when he had looked at her, and a wonderous warmth unfurled inside her.

He was doing it for *her*.

Unfortunately, she did not deserve it. She shut her eyes, her feelings in turmoil. She was grateful to him for doing it, but she was now more indebted to him than ever. It made her feel even worse.

The trickle of guilt was fast turning into a flood,

and she was in danger of drowning.

Chapter 6

Now that his fears over Mrs. Bennet's health were beginning to recede, Darcy turned his thoughts in another direction. He had spent over an hour yesterday afternoon with Mrs. Philips looking at lace, and that had been enough for a life-time. Any possibility that Elizabeth's aunt might improve upon further acquaintance had been squashed like a pancake. He could not categorically say that Mrs. Philips was the worst gossip he had ever known, but she came close.

That alone should have been enough to warn him away, but somehow, it was not. He told himself he was no longer needed, that he was free to leave. Yet still he lingered. He remembered Elizabeth's pallor and her uncertainty, and his heart would not allow it. There was still the chance that Mrs. Bennet's condition might deteriorate. Abandoning Elizabeth when her Papa was out of town was not an option. She needed a gentleman to help her.

Every time he considered living his life without

Elizabeth, he was inundated with such a feeling of emptiness that his mind skittered. It was not a decision that could be made on an impulse. He needed time to decide what to do.

It was also deucedly difficult to stop thinking about her, because if he did happen to forget her for a moment, Bingley would make some remark about the Bennets and bring all the images flooding back.

"Do you not think Miss Bennet is a perfect angel, Darcy?"

Darcy was bending down to take a shot in billiards, but he stopped short.

"I still think she smiles too much."

"There is no such thing as smiling too much. She is as radiant as a star, Darcy. At least she does not blow hot and cold like her sister Elizabeth. I find it impossible to determine what mood she is in. Miss Elizabeth is nice enough, but she is exhausting. I prefer someone more predictable."

Darcy was struck by that perspective.

"Do you really think Miss Elizabeth is changeable?"

"How could you not have noticed? One moment she is laughing, then she becomes vexed, and before you have had the chance to catch up, she turns rebellious. I do not understand her at all. Do you?"

"Strangely enough, I do."

"That is because you are more complicated than I am," said Bingley, affably. "My requirements are much simpler. You, Darcy, have always loved a challenge. It is something you enjoy. Whereas I am naturally lazy and cannot make the effort."

"Come Bingley, you do not fool me for a moment. You won a scholarship to Oxford because you were clever."

"Being clever and working hard are two different things. You must not mistake one for the other."

Darcy's lips twisted in amusement. "So I take it that you prefer Miss Bennet because she is *uncomplicated*. Does that mean you think her *simple*?"

"You knew very well that it is not what I meant," said Bingley, good naturedly. "Are you ever going to resume playing?"

Darcy took up the mace stick and set it against the ivory cue ball.

"I mean only that Miss Bennet is a joy to be around, and I am satisfied with that. If Miss Elizabeth suits you better, that is your problem."

Darcy was in the middle of taking his shot. It went wide, and Bingley threw his head back and laughed.

"What makes you think Miss Elizabeth suits me?" Darcy frowned. He was not going to encourage his friend to continue in this direction.

"I have known you for years, Darcy. I know you are the most fastidious man in the kingdom. So when I see you making overtures to a pretty young lady, I naturally draw my own conclusions. And when a gentleman who despises shopping is prepared to look at lace, then something is up. In other words, as you yourself admitted, I am clever enough to know what is happening in front of my very eyes."

"I am attracted to Elizabeth. I admit it." said Darcy. "She is a pretty young lady, so it is only natural."

Bingley was grinning from ear to ear.

"I do not see what is so amusing," said Darcy, severely.

"I do. You did not even realize that you were calling her Elizabeth. That tells me a great deal already."

Darcy was beginning to feel cornered by the direction of the conversation.

"I am doing my duty, that is all," he remarked. "Now if you could please take your turn, perhaps we will finally be able to focus on the game."

"It depends what game you are playing, my friend," said Bingley, and Darcy could have sworn his grin had become wider – if that were physically possible.

He had to resolve this issue with Elizabeth once and for all. Other people might start noticing, and that would not do. He needed to be more circumspect about how he behaved around her.

"If Mrs. Bennet is still feeling better," said Bingley, "I was thinking about inviting the Bennets to Netherfield tomorrow. If the weather is fine, we could spend some time outdoors, exploring the maze. What do you think?"

Darcy's heart lifted as he thought that he would see Elizabeth here at Netherfield.

"If I had my carriage," he replied, "I would say we should follow our original resolution and go to London, but we cannot. We will have to wait for Mr. Bennet to return."

"Exactly," said Bingley.

Darcy knew it was unwise. He knew he should object, but he could not bring himself to turn down an opportunity to spend time with Elizabeth.

A note was sent round to Longbourn that afternoon issuing an invitation, and a note was sent back promptly accepting the invitation.

They walked forward, surrounded by walls of green foliage, separated from everyone else. Darcy and Elizabeth might have been the only people in the world. As they turned a corner, they passed a stone bench. Darcy wondered how many lovers had occupied this bench before them, pretending to be lost, but seeking privacy. He sat down, then put out his hand to bring her next to him. She snuggled up to him, then turned her face up, her eyes dancing. He shut his eyes and placed his lips against hers just as her hands locked behind his head and drew him closer—.

"Mr. Darcy," said Evans, sliding the curtains open noisily. "You said to wake you up at ten."

Darcy groaned. His brain was groggy from lack of sleep. He had spent half the night struggling to fall asleep, and the other half struggling to wake up, plagued by visions that embarrassed him even while he was dreaming.

Then he remembered what day it was. He propped himself up on his elbow and peered through half-shut eyes at the window.

"What is the weather like? Is it raining?"

"It is a chilly day, sir, but I do not believe it will rain."

Darcy rolled onto his back. Thank heavens for that.

But Evans was wrong. An hour later, Darcy awoke to the patter of rain against the window, and he sprung up with an exclamation to stare down at the soggy lawn and the murky water that had pooled along the walkways.

Their maze excursion would have to be postponed. He knew it would probably just be put off until the following day, but he still felt bereft.

Then afternoon came, and patches of blue sky began to appear, and a pallid sun made an appearance. The grey puddles disappeared as if by magic, and hope rose up inside him.

Luck was on his side. Promptly at two, the Longbourn party appeared. Collins and Miss Bennet were on horseback, while the others were riding in an old farm cart that had certainly seen better days.

"Prepare yourself for the smell of hay and cow-dung," said Miss Bingley to Louisa, who laughed as though her sister had made the wittiest of jokes.

"Would you have preferred all the ladies to have six inches of mud on their petticoats?" said Darcy.

"I would have preferred it if they came in a proper carriage," she replied, "but I suppose that would be too much to expect."

Darcy ignored her. It would only encourage her if he answered. Instead, he went to the hallway as the Bennets entered, and took up his hat and great coat, ready to brave the maze.

Darcy had dreamt of spending time alone with Elizabeth, but nothing could be further from what his imagination had conjured up. Bingley and Jane set out ahead of everyone, followed by Miss Bingley and Mrs. Hurst.

To Mr. Darcy's dismay, however, Mr. Collins stuck like a burr to Elizabeth. Lydia followed closely, snagging her clothing from time to time on the well-trimmed hedges, and calling out to Mr. Collins to release her. Meanwhile, Mary plodded behind them, relating every detail of *The Odyssey* to Kitty, and showing off her elementary knowledge of Classical Greek by occasionally substituting a Greek word for English. This had the effect of having Collins stop and turn to correct her, holding up the whole party while he explained the rules of Greek grammar.

Finally, when Lydia managed to snag her sleeve for the third time, Darcy decided he could not bear it any longer. Trying not to snap irritably, Darcy turned to Mr. Collins so abruptly the clergyman crashed into him.

"I appreciate your desire to chaperon your cousins, Collins. However, the purpose of the maze is for everyone to spread out and find their own way. If we all walk together, it rather defeats the purpose."

Mr. Collins' eyes darted to Elizabeth then back to Darcy.

"Then I shall accompany Miss Elizabeth, and we will go in a different direction."

"Mr. Collins," said Elizabeth, putting a hand on the clergyman's sleeve. "I would be very obliged if you could watch over Lydia. She does not have a good sense of direction, and she will be immediately lost if you do not help her."

She gave Mr. Collins a quick smile. Mr. Collins looked as if he might object, but then thought better of it.

"Of course, Cousin Elizabeth. But you must promise me an opportunity to talk to you later. We have a conversation to continue."

"Actually," said Mary. "I was hoping Mr. Collins

would continue his explanation of the Greek tenses."

There was a fork in the maze. Darcy hooked his arm in Elizabeth's and steered her towards the left path. As soon as the others were out of sight, he let go of her, and began to run. Elizabeth ran after him, laughing, until they reached a bend in the maze. They stopped to listen. Darcy could still hear the others talking, but their voices were fading.

"I think we have lost them," he said.

She nodded, her eyes full of mischief. She looked enchanting.

"Thank goodness," she said. "Thank you for the rescue. Shall we continue on our way? I am eager to reach the middle of the maze before anyone else does."

That was not Darcy's plan at all. He hoped to spend as much time alone with Elizabeth in the maze, within the bounds of propriety, of course. But first, he asked the question that had been troubling him.

"I hope Mr. Collins is not scolding you and making your life difficult. Is that what he meant when he mentioned a conversation?"

Elizabeth's lips twitched. "No, it is not. Mr. Collins has asked me to marry him."

The words were a punch in the jaw, coming from nowhere.

"May I inquire what your answer was?"

He waited, motionless, terrified at what she would say next. His whole world hung in the balance.

"I gave none."

Her cheeks dimpled.

Darcy blinked at that enigmatic sentence. What did she mean? Was she actually considering marrying Mr. Collins? He waited for her to continue, but she said nothing else. The suspense made him wretched, but he could not very well continue with that line of questioning. He had already probed enough.

"I see," he replied.

"I wonder what it is you see, Mr. Darcy?" she said, her tone teasing. "Do you think it is a good match for me? There are those who believe I would be lucky to marry such a man."

This is not a laughing matter, he thought. *If you married him, my heart would crack like ice on a pond.*

He could not say that to her, so he stood tongue-tied, battling the nausea that churned inside him.

"Well, Mr. Darcy? What would you advise me to do?"

It occurred to him that she might be sounding him out, that this was a test to discover whether he cared about her. What would happen if he gave her an indication of his interest? How would she react?

It was out of the question. He would be leaving in a day or two at the most. Dreaming of the impossible would only increase his torment later. In any case, he had no intention of raising expectations he could not and would not fulfil.

"I do not believe for a moment that you are seriously asking me for advice, Miss Bennet," he said, striving for a lighter tone. "Nor do I flatter myself that you will follow any advice I give you, either."

Those delightful dimples made an appearance. "I thought it might be an opportunity to know you better, sir."

How those words struck a chord in his heart! He would give anything to get to know her better. Would she really like to know him?

He would bare his soul to her if she wished it.

Compelled by a pressing desire to tell her what he felt Darcy started to speak, but a loud shriek interrupted them, followed by high-pitched giggles.

It was Lydia Bennet. Naturally.

"I am lost!" cried Lydia. "Someone come and find me!"

Her unseemly behaviour poured cold water on his fervour. He was reminded now of the myriad reasons he could not allow himself to be attached to Elizabeth. He could *not* choose to know her better.

A sideways glance at Elizabeth revealed a scarlet stain on her cheeks. She was embarrassed at her sister's behaviour. Whatever tendency her younger sisters had towards vulgarity, Elizabeth did not share it.

"Pardon me if I am overstepping," he queried, "but I wonder why your parents did not engage a governess for your younger sisters?"

If anything, Elizabeth's blush grew deeper.

Darcy cursed himself for being such a fool. There was only one answer, of course. Financial considerations. Longbourn's coffers did not extend far enough.

"I beg your pardon," he said quickly, to cover the awkwardness of raising such an issue. "It is none of my concern."

If he were to marry Elizabeth, he could engage a governess for her sisters. He could help with the running of the estate, he could—

He could never marry Elizabeth Bennet.

"You are merely voicing what many people have wondered," she said, with a shrug. "The fact is, none of us had a governess. My parents were not overly attentive to these matters. They did not force us to learn the accomplishments we spoke about that night in Netherfield when I was staying here. I do not know if you recall our discussion about accomplished ladies."

Recall it? Darcy recalled it only too well. It was the day he had fallen in love with her. She had challenged his certainties and turned his world upside down.

"I do not have a clear answer," she continued. "Mama thinks Lydia is pretty enough to marry young – in which case a governess would be a waste -- and Papa thinks her too silly to be improved upon. Kitty is generally an afterthought."

He spotted the flaw in the argument at once.

"That does not explain why they did not hire a governess for *you*," he said emphatically, feeling indignant on her behalf at such neglect. Surely a young lady with so much natural aptitude deserved to have her abilities developed.

"True," she replied breezily, with no hint of resentment. "But I did not *need* a governess. I would have hated being told what to do. She would have tried to teach me useless things like painting tables, covering screens, and using the Globes. I would have escaped to the library whenever I had a chance so I could read Papa's books instead. I am quite as ungovernable as Lydia, you know."

How could Elizabeth compare herself to the empty-headed young miss whose shrill laughter could be heard across the maze?

"I can fully understand that a young lady such as yourself -- prompted by a curious and searching mind to read and discover more about the world -- would not wish to be hindered by a governess. I am not surprised you would chaff at the bit and avoid such restrictions. But the right governess might have developed some of the talents that you already possess."

"I found a way to develop the things I was interested in. I am not completely devoid of accomplishments, Mr. Darcy."

He raised his brow. "I never said you were."

"But you are bemoaning my lack of formal schooling."

"Now you are choosing to misunderstand me."

Darcy hesitated. Then, because he could not

help himself, he added, "As it so happens, I agree with you. It *would* have been a great pity if a governess had dampened your independent spirit."

She looked at him in surprise, her beautiful dark eyes widening. For once she was at a loss for words. Pleased that he had managed to fluster her, Darcy smiled openly.

Elizabeth returned his smile. This time her gaze did not hold a challenge. It was open and sincere, and he felt his walls crumble.

Now it was *his* turn to be flustered. His mouth dried up and his heart began to drum forcefully.

"Why, Mr. Darcy!" she said, "I did not know you approved of my uncivilized ways."

Her voice was teasing, openly flirtatious.

"I—of course I approve of you, Miss Bennet."

At this moment, he approved of everything about her. He could not recall a single reason for not asking her to marry him then and there. She was perfection itself.

It would be such a relief to stop struggling and simply let it all out. He wanted desperately to tell her how ardently he admired her and be done with it.

A wild impulse seized him. He would do it. He would propose.

"We have taken a wrong turn," she remarked.

Darcy was so engrossed in his own quandary, he did not understand what she was saying. Had Elizabeth read his mind and was warning him not to proceed?

He felt bewildered and horribly, wretchedly disappointed.

"A wrong turn?" he repeated, his voice sounding hoarse.

"Yes, Mr. Darcy. We will have to retrace our steps. We have reached a dead end in the maze."

He stared at the tall hedge blocking their way and began to laugh, weakly at first, then from his belly, a deep grumbling laugh that he would never have expected from himself. Meanwhile, Elizabeth stood watching him with puzzled amusement.

Elizabeth had just saved him from making the biggest mistake in his life, but he did not know whether he was laughing from relief or despair.

"So we have, Miss Elizabeth. So we have. Let us see if we can make our way back."

He had come close to the abyss, and luck had intervened to make certain he would not do anything foolish.

The voices of all his relations flitted through his head like ghosts, clamoring against him. Many of them *were* ghosts. His mother, Lady Anne, a pale recollection in his mind; his father's image, proud and demanding; the grandfather he had never met whose portrait had terrified him as a child; a knight in armor, looking down at him in the portrait gallery; a courtier in King Henry's VIII's court.

The procession of specters passed in front of his eyes, accusing him of sullying the family name. Then came the people who were alive. Lord and Lady Matlock; his cousin the viscount with his cold and distant wife; Lady Catherine, and Colonel Fitzwilliam -- the only cousin he might count on to support him. Everyone was accusing him of failing in his duty.

Nevertheless, even with all those voices clamoring for his attention, he could not resist spending what little time he would have with her.

If he did not find his way out soon, he would be lost forever.

"We need to find a way out," said Elizabeth.

Darcy started and stared at her, his eyes like a turbulent sea. She would have liked to avoid his gaze, but she was caught in it as she strove to decipher his mood.

"Miss Bennet, you have guessed my thoughts."

She would have thought it was obvious; they were lost in the maze. Yet his intense scrutiny hinted at something else entirely. It made her aware that they were in an enclosed space and that she could no longer hear the others.

She was alone with Mr. Darcy, and his eyes were hungry.

She shivered.

"Are you cold?" he said. "Let me give you my coat."

"I am not cold." She was feeling almost feverish.

"I would not have you become ill."

He peeled off his coat. In the falling dusk, his outline against the sky was dark and masculine. He came forward to drape his coat over her shoulders, and his breath fanned her neck. Her skin responded with a cascade of goosebumps that sizzled then died down when he moved away.

"Is that better?"

"Yes," she said. The coat still harbored the heat from his body. His musky scent settled around her, enveloping her in a snug shield against the cold.

He moved to stand before her. His gaze dropped to her mouth, and she stopped breathing. Did he mean to kiss her? Did she want him to? She stared, mesmerized, as his head tilted towards her, and his lips approached hers. She stood unmoving, her pulse throbbing in her ears.

It was the barest of touches, soft silk against the tender skin of her lips. Yet it reached into every inch of her. She pressed forward, not entirely certain what to expect, but needing more.

Then it crossed her mind that she had not told

Mr. Darcy about Mama. Her troubled conscience rose between them like a ghost, and she stopped cold.

He would not kiss her if he knew. She was sure of it.

She pushed away, putting a distance between them, working to catch her breath and sooth her wayward senses.

"Miss Elizabeth," he said, his voice unfamiliar and rasping. "I am sorry. That was unforgivable."

"We need to get out." She repeated what she had already said, because it was hard to come up with anything else. "The others have all gone."

He blinked, and looked mortified.

"I am sorry. I—" He cleared his throat. "Yes, we do need to find our way out. It is almost dark."

It gave Elizabeth a goal she could latch onto, something to distract her from the riotous feelings gripping her. She desperately needed to get back to the others because she was anxious to clear her mind. She no longer knew what she was doing.

She was half in love with Mr. Darcy. She had lost her direction, in more ways than one.

To her relief, it did not take them long to find their way out after all. Fortunately, they could gauge their direction by the light at the front of the house, which kept them oriented. They spoke only when necessary.

As they emerged from the looming dark hedges to the end of the path that led to the house, Elizabeth stopped and took off his coat. He busied himself putting it on, not looking at her.

She shared his embarrassment. At some point, she would think about what just happened and what it meant, but for now, she had something else on her mind. As long as there were secrets between them, she could never give herself permission to explore how she felt about him.

She would have to unburden herself. It was too late now. The others would be waiting for them, but she would do so at the earliest opportunity, and nothing would stop her. He would consider it very forward of her to propose a meeting, but that was the least of her worries.

"Mr. Darcy, I was wondering if you were planning to go walking tomorrow after the morning service. I would like to consult you about something."

Mr. Darcy broke his stride and gave a little stumble.

She could not help it. She laughed, and with the laughter, most of her tension disappeared.

"Surely, Mr. Darcy, the prospect of walking with me does not merit a fall? It cannot be as terrible as that."

A smile skimmed over his lips. She watched it,

fascinated. He could be so charming if he made the effort.

"I know by now that you often express opinions that are not your own."

There was an odd note in his voice she had never heard before.

She regretted her comment. She was misleading him. There was nothing playful about their meeting tomorrow.

"On the contrary, sir," she said, seriously. "I mean every word. You will understand tomorrow."

"Now I am doubly intrigued. I cannot imagine any situation in which the prospect would be anything but delightful."

He was going to be disappointed. She shrugged inwardly. She would worry about it tomorrow. For now, she did not mind seeming just a little bit mysterious. She liked the idea of leaving him to puzzle over what she wanted to say.

She might as well enjoy it while she could. It was not going to last. She could guess all too well what his reaction would be.

"Well then, Mr. Darcy, do not say that I did not warn you."

"You have given me fair warning, Miss Elizabeth."

It occurred to her that she ought not to have implied that she and Mr. Darcy would be walking to Meryton alone.

"I hope you will bring Mr. Bingley along with you. I intend to bring my sisters."

They had reached the door. As it opened, she felt him stiffen.

"Oh, there you are Mr. Darcy," drawled Miss Bingley. "We were preparing to send out a search party for you. The others are eager to return to Longbourn. They have been awaiting Miss Eliza this half-hour."

In the bright light of the candles, Mr. Darcy's face was shuttered.

"As you can see, we are back, safe and sound."

The tension was palpable.

"Oh, you are too late, Lizzy," said Lydia, wandering into the hallway. "Mr. Collins has already agreed to ride with me on the box seat. You will have to sit at the back."

As the others joined them, Elizabeth's stomach was churning like a waterwheel, her emotions in disarray. Tomorrow, everything was going to come tumbling down.

Chapter 7

The next day was Sunday, and the party from Netherfield and the party from Longbourn met at church. Mr. Bingley's sisters showed no interest in going for a walk, saying that, with all the shops closed, there was nothing to do in Meryton, and that it was too windy on Oakham Mount. Mr. Hurst proposed a game of cards, but no one took him up on it, and the two groups soon went their own way.

Elizabeth was dreading the encounter with Darcy. Not only did she have an unpleasant duty ahead of her, but she was doing her utmost not to dwell on what had happened last night.

Her efforts were in vain. As soon as Mr. Darcy drew close, Elizabeth's sight was drawn to his lips, and a vivid memory of the sensations they had evoked washed over her. Heat flooded into her face, and she hastily lowered her eyes. Chiding herself, she resolved not to look in Mr. Darcy's direction until she had achieved her objective.

On his part, Mr. Darcy appeared to have reverted

to his old manner. He was silent and arrogant. She should have found that more daunting, but she welcomed it instead. At least with *that* Mr. Darcy, she knew where she stood.

Fortunately, there was no opportunity for them to talk privately at the beginning. The conversation was a group affair that was quickly becoming strained. Lydia and Mary were vying for Mr. Collins' attention; Mr. Collins kept turning his head to address Elizabeth; Kitty was looking sullen because she felt overlooked; and Mr. Darcy was growing grimmer by the moment.

Mr. Bingley and Jane were the only ones who did not join in. They were walking silently side by side, wrapped in a world of their own.

It was not long, however, before Elizabeth's younger sisters were walking ahead. Lydia and Mary were each holding on to one of Mr. Collins' arms, practically pulling him with them, with Kitty trying to keep up. Jane and Mr. Bingley had slowed down, trying to put some distance between the noisy group ahead. It meant that Elizabeth and Mr. Darcy had to walk at almost a crawl to put a gap between them and the rest.

Mr. Darcy embarked on a commendable attempt to maintain a civil conversation.

"How is your mother's health today, Miss Elizabeth?"

"Much improved, sir," she replied, blushing to the roots of her hair. In a few minutes he would discover that practically every word she was uttering was a lie.

"The path in this direction is very pleasant, is it not, Miss Elizabeth?"

"Very pleasant indeed," she replied, absently. She was desperately trying to think of a good way to introduce the topic. She had rehearsed what to say, but that did not make it any easier. There was really no way to bring it up, other than blurting it out.

"And the weather is particularly mild for this time of the year."

"Very much so," she said. "But—"

"I have something for you, Miss Elizabeth," he said, with a meaningful look. "I am fully aware it is improper for a gentleman to give a young lady a gift, so do not think of it this way. I do not want the lace to go to waste. It is the result of my shopping expedition with your aunt two days ago."

"But your sister--?"

The corner of his mouth twitched. "My sister has no need of lace at present. She is in Town."

"And can acquire something better?"

"Something like that," he acknowledged. "But this is a fine sample, or I would not be giving it to you."

He took out a small package that had been folded small enough to fit in his pocket. It was wrapped in brown paper that looked the worse for wear.

No doubt it was beautiful lace. She tempted, but given what she was about to say to him, she could not possibly accept such an expensive purchase. She was sorry that he had wasted his money.

"Now that you mention it, Mr. Darcy, I have been meaning to thank you for drawing away my aunt, sir. It must have been an ordeal to spend so much time with her discussing the merits of lace."

"Not at all, Miss Bennet. It was a simple matter. I just asked for the most expensive lace to be had, and Mrs. Philips helped me select one out of the three possibilities."

She looked down at the package in his extended hand.

"It is not proper to accept such a gift," she said.

She sounded unnaturally prim, and Mr. Darcy looked baffled.

"My reasons will soon be apparent," she hastened, seeking to justify her refusal. "I have something particular I want to say."

Without conscious thought, he stopped and thrust the package back into his pocket. They were facing each other. His expression was so solicitous, it only made matters much worse.

Elizabeth wavered. She did not know if she had the courage to face him.

"I hope you will hear me out before casting judgement."

"Of course."

She quaked in her shoes, but the time for indecision was over. "I have a confession to make, Mr.

Darcy," she said, trying to sound playful, but failing miserably. "This is very difficult for me."

Darcy fixed his attention on her in a most unsettling way. He seemed to be expecting something specific. Perhaps he already knew about Mama. Why must he be so intense?

"I am all ears," he said, his voice sounding husky.

Darcy's heart was thumping. This was the moment. She meant to give him an indication that she would welcome his attention. Tradition dictated that the gentleman should introduce such a topic, but he liked the idea of Elizabeth initiating it. She was uninhibited, and he treasured that quality in her.

He could scarcely wait to hear what she was about to say. He longed for it with all his heart. His hands trembled with anticipation. Already he was searching around him for somewhere more hidden where he could show her the extent of his -- appreciation.

"You cannot imagine how I have struggled," she said. "You must allow me to tell you the truth."

It was the prelude to her revelation. There could be no doubt of it. His pulse galloped, his mouth grew dry, his heart felt like it would burst.

"The fact is, Mr. Darcy, Mama does not suffer from apoplexy. It was an excuse she used to stop Mr. Collins from proposing to me. It got out of hand when Mr. Collins enlisted your help."

Darcy's mind fumbled to make sense of her words. They were so different from what he had expected, he simply could not comprehend them. He could not believe his ears. Standing in the middle of the pathway, he tried to gather his senses into something coherent.

"I beg your pardon, Miss Elizabeth, but I am afraid I did not hear what you just said."

Her face scarlet, she looked down at a clump of grass in the middle of the footpath. He examined it as well, seeking illumination. Her words finally started to penetrate through the fog in his skull.

She had not intended to tell him she cared for him. That was his first comprehensible thought. She did *not* care for him.

The next realization followed quickly after. She had *lied*.

It hit him with the force of a hammer. Rocking under the impact, he did something uncivil. He left her on the path without taking his leave and marched quickly away, not knowing nor caring where he was going.

Darcy stared out over a landscape he had come to love because of *her*. It was grim and desolate with winter frost. There was no joy in it anymore.

How ridiculous he had been, to have expected so much of her. What on earth had possessed him to think that she was going to make such an intimate revelation?

She did not love him. The words were like ash, bleak and dead. And he was a fool. He had completely misunderstood her.

Finally, the meaning of what she had said sank in, and fury flared up like a flame inside him. Darcy had been deliberately and consciously *fooled.*

Elizabeth had not only lied. She had been *lying* to him. Bared-faced lies that had gone on for the last six days. His heart clenched and squeezed. It was the worst thing she could have done because he had never seen it coming.

He had never once in his long catalog of objections to their marriage listed duplicity as one of her faults. If anything, it was the opposite. He had always considered that, with her outspoken and direct manner, she would find it hard to survive the convoluted world of upper-class Society.

When he first arrived in Meryton, he had been jaded and cynical. He believed that all young ladies were like Caroline Bingley: plotting, scheming, and flattering their way into a gentleman's affections. Young ladies, he thought, were all the same, decked up in demure white muslin and sparkling jewels, but with only one purpose in their lives – how to weasel their way into his heart.

Elizabeth Bennet was a breath of fresh air in a world of stale, overcrowded ballrooms where young ladies never revealed who they were. With her candid gaze, her unpretentious manners, and refusal to ingratiate herself with him, Elizabeth was a dream come true, a true partner of the mind and soul. She was sharp, alive with an intelligence that teased and sparkled. She had enchanted him by refusing to play the role society thrust on her.

He had trusted her unequivocally, and she had played him like a fool. She was as bad as all the others, only she was more devious, because he had been taken off-guard. The impish smile, the flirtatious way she challenged and confronted him – it was all nothing but a façade.

He could never let her know that he had allowed her into his heart. And to think that yesterday in the maze, he had almost declared his love! He had even been reckless enough to kiss her.

Thank goodness he had discovered the truth before it was too late. Darcy could now leave Netherfield without a moment's hesitation. Eventually, he would remember this time with her only because it brought him the misery of knowing that there was no such thing as truth and honesty in this world.

But before he left, he would give her a piece of his mind. He would not keep silent over her treachery.

He strode back to where he had left Elizabeth. She was still standing on the path, looking distraught. Her face was drained of color, he noticed with a sense of satisfaction. He hoped she was suffering as much as he was. But there was little chance of that.

"I am truly sorry, sir," she said. "I would have told you sooner, but I could not betray Mama."

"So you chose to betray *me*," he said, teeth gritted, his jaw aching with the effort not to rant and shout.

"Mama is my family, sir. You are a stranger."

A stranger. That was all Darcy was to her. She had no idea of the stabbing pain those words brought him.

"I wonder why you did not send me away when I came to your assistance, since I am nothing but a stranger?"

"You may recall, Mr. Darcy, that I *did* try to discourage you, but you were most persistent."

And he had stupidly believed he was doing her a good turn!

"So, you are telling me that while Mr. Bingley and I were running around trying to help you out, you were all laughing at us, secure in the knowledge that Mrs. Bennet was perfectly well."

"Not laughing, sir. Never that. If you knew how much my conscience—"

"It mattered nothing to you that I took on the expense of sending a carriage for Mr. Bennet?"

She looked away. He was putting her to shame, and he was *glad* of it. Let her feel *something*, even if it was nothing compared to the anguish he was experiencing.

He ignored the part of him that was aghast at his conduct.

"Papa will repay you. I will see to it."

She was offering coin, adding insult to injury.

"I do not need your paltry money," he answered in clipped tones, her words incensing him more. "You cannot buy your way out of this. You cannot ease your conscience – if it actually exists. How am I to believe anything you say. Do you even begin to understand the depth of your treachery?"

She was silent, her eyes averted, drawing a line in the ground with the point of her half-boot. He noticed that the tip of her boot was encrusted with mud. She was careless with everything, including her own clothes. Stupidly, he had found that carelessness appealing, an indication of her free spirit.

Her face was hidden in the shadow cast by her bonnet. It frustrated him not to see her expression and know what she was feeling. What if she was secretly laughing at him for being so easily duped?

"Do you have anything to say for yourself?" he prompted, hoping to rile her up so she would say something. "Or are you so hardened in your practiced deception that you have encountered situations like this before?"

She looked up then, and her eyes flashing with the defiance Darcy had always admired. Even now, he was charmed by the fire in her eyes.

Hating himself for his weakness, he steeled his expression into the usual shield of arrogance he wore against the world.

"I do not know what you expect me to say, Mr. Darcy," she said, in a quiet, thin voice. "The situation was not of my choosing. I could not expose Mama to ridicule after word began to spread of her illness."

"Do you think I had not taken Mrs. Bennet's measure already? She has made herself ridiculous from the very first day I encountered her."

The tightening of her expression told him that he was going too far by insulting Mrs. Bennet, but he would not abandon his blunt manner of speaking to spare her feelings. Unlike Elizabeth Bennet, Darcy told the truth.

"If you had such a poor opinion of us," she said, coldly, "then I am surprised you condescended to spend any time with us at all. You have confirmed what I suspected all along—that whenever you were lurking silently in the corners— which was most of the time—your sole intention was to find fault with us."

When had he ever *lurked* in the corners? If he had *lurked*, it had been because he had been foolhardy enough to harbor feelings for her. He was tempted to tell her so, to make her realize how much she had lost through her villainy, but he would not humiliate himself further.

Instead, he went on the attack.

"So it is for this—this utterly ridiculous reason —that we were compelled to stay at Netherfield instead of leaving for London as we planned?"

Her eyes widened. Darcy pressed on. Now that he knew what she was like, he had no scruples informing her some plain truths himself. If they were hurtful, then she only had herself to blame.

"Mr. Bingley and his sisters are planning to close up Netherfield for the winter and to stay in Town," he said icily. "Mr. Bingley and I intended to leave the day after the ball. We were on the verge of doing so when Mrs. Bennet was taken sick."

The Longbourn ladies would discover now that their machinations had failed. He would ensure that Bingley escaped the trap they had set to ensnare him.

"Indeed?" She raised her brow. "I am sorry to hear the events of the last few days have inconvenienced you. Do you intend to stay long in town?"

Her voice had a hard edge to it.

"Very long," said Darcy. "The house will be shut down completely. I do not believe Mr. Bingley intends to come back again."

There, thought Darcy full of self-righteous dignity. *That ought to put her in her place.*

She put up her chin and looked straight at him for the first time since her revelation. "Do you mean to say that, while Mr. Bingley has been singling my sister Jane out for particular attention, exposing her to gossip, and making her care for him, he was already planning to leave and never return?"

"Yes!" said Darcy, without thinking, his words like a rapier, cutting and hacking.

Then, as the implication of her words sank in. "No!"

He realized too late that he had fallen into a trap of his own devising. He could not say that Bingley was genuinely attached to Jane, because then Bingley would be unable to extricate himself. Yet he could not blacken his friend's name by implying that Bingley was a heartless scoundrel who had flirted with Jane, then abandoned her.

He had landed himself in a pickle.

"*We* may have been guilty of an innocent deception that went amiss," she said, in that same hard voice. "That is *nothing* compared with a young gentleman choosing to toy with a lady's affections for his own amusement."

Darcy knew on some level she was right, but he had no way to explain the situation to her without revealing his friend's true feelings. Besides, his anger was still burning. Fueled by the acrid sting of disillusionment, he lashed out.

"At least Mr. Bingley did not tell outright lies."

"No, he did far worse," responded Elizabeth. "He deviously concealed the truth. He is doing so at this very minute."

He looked ahead to where Mr. Bingley and Miss Bennet were walking, their shoulders almost touching as they leaned towards each other.

"You think Bingley devious?" he countered. "When your mother has been putting all her energy into ensnaring him? If anyone is guilty of exposing your sister to the censor of her friends and acquaintances, it is your mother, who has been bragging to all and sundry that Bingley is about to offer for Miss Bennet. Or you might blame Miss Bennet herself, for using her smiles to lure Bingley into complacency."

He was breathing heavily, furious and desperate at the same time. She winced as his words hit their mark. He felt fully justified and more than pleased with himself for scoring a point. A part of him sensed that by blaming Miss Bennet, he had gone too far.

"And how do you explain that—episode in the maze yesterday? Was I using my smiles to entrap you as well? Were you an innocent victim?"

The words shook him to the core. "What?" he said, bewildered. "No—how could you think—?"

He was rocked off balance, reduced to stuttering.

"You have said more than enough, Mr. Darcy." Her voice was like the north wind, chilling him to the bone. "I believed you both to be gentlemen, but now I see I have been misled. I should have trusted my first impressions. From the beginning, from the very first moment, your manners impressed me with the fullest belief of your arrogance, your conceit, and your selfish disdain of the feelings of others. You and your friend, sir, have taken advantage of us. *You* are the ones guilty of treachery. Do not blame us. Look to yourselves."

She turned and started to walk back towards Longbourn, then stopped.

"Kindly inform my sisters that I am indisposed, and that we *all* need to return home."

Without another word, she set down the path.

As she left, she took all Darcy's anger with her. Without it, the despair he was holding back came flooding in, leaving him without the strength to stand. Staggering towards the fallen remains of a tree trunk, he sank down and idly watched a line of ants scurrying around, carrying a treasure to their home. He envied the mindless toil that kept them too occupied to experience unhappiness.

He could not bring himself to move.

You are the ones guilty of treachery.

Darcy had kissed her. If someone had come upon them, Elizabeth would have been compromised. And now she believed he was toying with her, that he was devoid of honor.

How could he have made such a mess of it all? He felt wrung out, deprived of all strength. He did not know if he would ever be able to stand up again.

"I say, Darcy."

Darcy raised his head and found Bingley and

Miss Bennet peering down at him. "Are you unwell?"

The sight of Bingley's unsuspecting expression rekindled Darcy's anger at being duped. Somehow, Elizabeth had made him forget that aspect of the situation. He could never forgive her for what she had done. Bingley thought Miss Bennet an angel, but she had been deceiving him. Should he blurt out the truth about Mrs. Bennet's illness? Surely Bingley deserved to know.

I believed you both to be gentlemen.

Elizabeth may not consider him a gentleman, but he would not do such an ungentlemanly thing, not in front of Miss Bennet. He was not so lost to propriety. He would wait until the two men were in Netherfield and talk to Bingley privately.

Bingley put out a hand to him.

"Do you need help standing up? Has Miss Elizabeth gone for help?"

"It is nothing. A momentary weakness," Darcy replied. The concern on Bingley's face reminded him of how Elizabeth had taken his concern for her and spat it in his face.

Another surge of anger swept through him. It gave him the push he needed to jerk to his feet.

"Miss Elizabeth is indisposed. She would like us all to turn back. If you could call the others, Bingley?"

Darcy would make sure Bingley did not spend another moment with Miss Bennet. The very sight of the Bennet sisters sickened him. He hoped never to set eyes on them again. It was a very good thing this had happened. It gave Darcy the much-needed incentive he had been lacking.

He would depart at dawn and never set foot in the neighborhood again in his life.

Chapter 8

Odious man, thought Elizabeth, odious, dis-
agreeable, arrogant man! And he believed
himself a gentleman? Ha! At least she had the
satisfaction of telling Darcy her opinion of him.

She ran down the path, a feeling of outrage
choking her. Once she was out of sight, she stopped
and gave vent to her frustration by kicking at a log.

She regretted it instantly as pain shot up
through her toe and up her leg. She hopped about on
one foot, groaning. *Bother, bother, bother!* If she ended
up not being able to walk properly for the rest of her
life, it would all be Mr. Darcy's fault.

When she had envisioned telling him the truth,
she had not expected that he would react quite that
way. Obviously, she did not think he would be happy
to know that he had been tricked, but she had not anticipated the poisonous words he had uttered.

They had wounded her to the core. How dare he
pass judgement in that pompous, supercilious way?
How could he insult her and her family so completely,

assuming the worse, when he had not even *asked* to hear the whole story? And then to accuse Jane of all people, who did not have a deceitful bone in her body! Jane, who loved Bingley with all her big heart. Jane who had always been uncertain of Mr. Bingley's affection, and now it turned out she was justified. The insufferable Mr. Darcy had admitted that he and Mr. Bingley were planning to leave Netherfield for London without a backward glance.

That had been the final straw. He had *kissed* her yesterday. She had tried and tried not to think about it, not to give it any importance. Admittedly, it had not been a big kiss – a mere peck, to be precise. She did not want to make too much of it, but young ladies had been forced to marry for less.

And today, without the slightest bit of remorse, he had announced that he did not have the least intention of staying. How very fortunate she had stopped him and not allowed him any further liberties. Because there were not two ways about it. He had deceived her. He may not have promised her anything, he may have not meant anything by kissing her, but he had not told her they were about to abandon ship, either.

It had been a terrible mistake to tell him the truth. How naïve she had been to think a man like Darcy – who did not have an honest bone in his body – deserved to hear the truth. A man who did not care a fig for her.

Elizabeth felt all her energy drain out of her

with a whoosh. She still felt angry at Mr. Darcy, but she also felt angry at herself. She had humiliated herself completely, and for what? She had told him the truth and he had kicked her in the teeth with it.

There was a tree stump to the side of the path. She sank down onto it, tucking her skirts around her to protect herself. It was a miserably cold day, especially now that she was no longer walking. She was shivering.

Why had she done it? That was the question that was beginning to haunt her now. Had Mr. Darcy's good opinion been so important, that she had been willing to jeopardize Jane's chances?

She had not known that Jane did not actually have any chances.

The fact was Mr. Darcy's kindness over the last few days had softened her towards him. She had felt a taste of what it meant to be safeguarded by a gentleman with the means to accomplish whatever he desired. She had felt safe. She had never had that feeling before.

It was not only that. She had to be honest with herself. Her whole body stirred at the memory of him drawing her into his arms. In that instant, she had thrown all caution to the wind. If it were not for the intervention of her dratted conscience, she did not know what might have happened. When did she start to see him differently? It had happened so suddenly over the last few days that she had not even noticed.

She was in love with Mr. Darcy.

Tears sprang up to burn her eyes. What was she to do? It was all too late. He was leaving, and she would never see him again.

She stared through blurry eyes at a group of ants trying to carry a colossal chunk of food to their home. They were doing their best to share the burden, but they kept dropping it. She wished she could reach down and help them, but she knew they would run away if she tried to do it.

She wiped away her tears angrily with her sleeve. The hard surface of the stump was digging through her clothes and the cold was seeping into every pore. She took hold of a branch and pulled herself up. If she did not go home soon, she might catch her death of a cold. Part of her wanted that to happen. If she became sick and died, it would serve Mr. Darcy right.

The childish reflection did not last long. The cold reality was that Mr. Darcy would not even know about it, because he would be long gone.

She did not wish to die of a cold. She was not prepared to sacrifice herself in the hope that Mr. Darcy would regret his harsh words.

There was a silver lining in the whole sorry business. She had accomplished something very important by making her confession. She had discovered Mr. Bingley's infamous plans. She would have to set in motion a plan to lower her sister's expectations so she could protect Jane from heartbreak.

Never mind that her own heart was in danger of shattering.

∞∞∞

Elizabeth took a circuitous route to Longbourn. She wanted to avoid any chance coming face to face with Darcy again, and the long walk helped her get her agitation under control.

She arrived at Longbourn to an unexpected discovery. Mr. Bennet had come home. It was a wonderful surprise. She had never been so glad to see him in her life.

"What is wrong with your eyes, Lizzy?" he said, coming into the hallway as she untied her bonnet and took off her cloak. "They are all red. You have not been crying, have you?"

He was teasing her, of course. He did not really expect her to be crying.

"You know very well I am not the crying type," she said with a half-sob, and threw herself into her father's arms. "I am just glad you are back."

Mr. Bennet patted her on the back awkwardly. "I would have arranged to go away more frequently, if I knew I would be missed so much."

He set her at arm's length and examined her. Somehow, she managed to muster a smile. "Now you must tell me what you have been up to."

"You will not believe what has happened," she said.

"I know exactly what has happened." Papa was looking amused. "Mrs. Bennet has been explaining it to me this last half-hour. Needless to say, I am extremely annoyed at being brought from my dying friend's bedside for such a trivial matter. However, upon reflection, there are enough advantages to the situation to overcome my annoyance. Travelling back in such a luxurious style was one of them."

"Whatever do you mean, Papa?" she asked.

"A journey in Mr. Darcy's coach, with the best horses awaiting me at some of the best inns – all on Mr. Darcy's credit. It is not an experience I can easily forget."

She gasped. This made everything even worse.

"Oh, tell me Mr. Darcy did not send his own personal carriage for you! He asked for your direction to send an express. I never imagined he would go so far! And that you would come. Did you even read my letter?"

"I did," he said, "but it would have been very ungrateful not to accept Mr. Darcy's offer, now that the carriage was there."

"I am sorry, Papa. I did what I could."

She was angry all over again at Mama's tangle. All this was because Lydia had taken it into her mind to marry Mr. Collins.

"You need not look so dismayed, Lizzy. For a

gentleman with his wealth, the expense is nothing to him. However, I do dislike putting myself in anyone's debt. I will have to offer to reimburse him, I suppose."

Elizabeth sank into a chair. *I do not want your paltry money.*

"Yes, you must, Papa. Mr. Darcy is now aware fully of the circumstances."

"He discovered it, then? Well, well. I am hardly surprised. Your mother's acting skills leave much to be desired. She could never make a living on the stage."

"He did not discover it, Papa. I informed him."

Mr. Bennet stared at her in astonishment.

"Why on earth would you do such a thing?" he said. "You should have kept him in his ignorance. It would have been excellent sport to see him bamboozled, especially after the way he treated you. What came into you?"

It was a good question, and unfortunately she already knew the answer. She felt despondent all over again.

"I do hope this debacle will not drive Mr. Bingley away."

Elizabeth shook her head.

"You need not be afraid of that," she replied bitterly. "Mr. Bingley cannot be driven away, because he already intended to give up Netherfield."

"Are you certain, Lizzy? I had thought him a more honorable gentleman than that."

"I am certain. Mr. Darcy informed me."

"Ah. It all seems to come down to Mr. Darcy."

"Well, you could hardly expect me to tell the truth to Mr. Bingley."

"I do not understand why you decided to tell the truth to either of them. You are not usually such a goose."

Elizabeth looked down. She already regretted her impulse at confession. She did not need Papa to tell her so. She had given Mr. Darcy even more of an excuse to look down his nose at them. He was despicable.

Mr. Bennet reached out and tucked his finger under Elizabeth's chin.

"I hope you are not harboring some foolish infatuation towards Mr. Darcy, child."

His voice was gentle.

She pushed Mr. Bennet's hand away and swirled round.

"Infatuation? Towards Mr. Darcy? I *despise* the man. He is the most loathsome creature in the world. If he was the last man in the world, I would not consider marrying him."

"A pity," said Mr. Bennet. "He would have suited you perfectly, with his grim and disdainful manner."

"It is not at all funny, Papa." She was close to bursting into tears. "You do not know half the things he said about me – about us all."

"I can imagine them all too clearly. No gentleman as proud as Darcy would want to look like a fool. But let us come back to that other matter. What did he say about Bingley?"

"Just that they had already planned to close the house after the Netherfield Ball and did not anticipate returning any time soon."

Mr. Bennet sighed. "I am indeed sorry to hear that, Lizzy. I was convinced Mr. Bingley was interested in our Jane, but that is what these grand gentlemen are like. They do whatever they wish and never answer to the consequences."

"Can you do nothing, Papa? Can you not speak to him? Force him to think of the repercussions for Jane?"

"I suppose I could challenge him to a duel."

"Be serious, Papa."

"If you do not wish me to fight a duel, I will go to Netherfield and explain to both gentlemen that my daughters are in love with them, and that Mr. Bingley must not depart any time soon. No young lady likes to be crossed in love, and it would be heartless of Mr. Bingley to do so."

"I wish you would not be facetious for once. It is a serious matter. You cannot make Jane's feelings the butt of your jokes. It will break her heart if Mr. Bingley leaves." She registered what else he had said. "And, for your information, I am *not* in love with Mr. Darcy. Quite the opposite."

"I would say good riddance to them both, except that I must indeed ride over to speak to Mr. Darcy. If they are intending to leave soon, I need to discharge my debt as quickly as possible. Honor dictates it."

Elizabeth groaned. It was humiliating for Papa to be obliged to go, cap in hand, to reimburse Mr. Darcy Her cheeks burned at what Mr. Darcy would think, but she could not prevent Papa from going. Men were very touchy about matters of honor.

At that moment the door opened, and the rest of the walking party stepped into the house. Elizabeth listened intently, praying that Mr. Darcy and Mr. Bingley were not planning to come in. The only one talking was Lydia, who was offering tea to Mr. Collins.

She spotted her father, gave a small squeal, and ran over to give him a quick embrace.

"Hello Papa! Back already?"

Mr. Bennet did not have a chance to answer before she turned back to focus her attention on Mr. Collins. "Do you like to hold tea parties, Mr. Collins? I love to play hostess to our neighbors. What is your favorite type of cake?"

To Elizabeth's relief, there were no visitors. Mary was the last one in. Elizabeth bit back the impulse to ask her what had happened to Mr. Darcy.

Meanwhile, Mr. Bennet was watching Lydia with astonished irony.

"So that's the way things are, I see," said Mr. Bennet as Lydia and Collins passed into the parlor.

"It is because of Lydia that this whole debacle happened."

"Mrs. Bennet told me so, but I did not think Lydia capable of carrying it through. I am pleasantly surprised. Perhaps it will do Lydia some good to behave herself for once. She might even make a habit of it."

"Not once she gets what she wishes for," said Lizzy. "I am not even sure she can keep it up long enough to convince Mr. Collins."

"Well, well, we shall see."

Elizabeth heard Jane's voice in the hallway speaking to Hill. She still had not made up her mind whether to tell Jane about Mr. Bingley's imminent departure.

"Could you please not say anything to Jane yet about Bingley's departure, Papa?"

"You have told the truth to Darcy, but you will not tell it to your sister? I am quite shocked. I must retreat to the library to meditate on the folly of human beings. I am finding the situation excessively diverting."

It was not until later in the afternoon, when Mr. Collins had retired to the library to read a book, that Elizabeth and Jane had a chance to talk.

"Where did you disappear to, Lizzy? I am very sorry I left you with Mr. Darcy. Did he say anything that offended you."

He had said a great deal that offended her.

"I am sorry I left so suddenly," said Elizabeth, "I hope it did not cause any awkwardness."

"Not at all. I am ashamed to admit it, but I barely noticed." Jane's ears were red.

"So," said Elizabeth, "how was your walk with Mr. Bingley? I hope nothing untoward transpired."

The glow on Jane's face spoke volumes.

If he was taking advantage of her poor sister, Elizabeth would find some way to pay him back. She would follow him to the end of the world and make sure he got his just deserts for doing this.

"Oh, no, nothing untoward," said Jane. "He is a perfect gentleman."

Not quite as perfect as you think, thought Elizabeth.

"Well? Are you going to tell me all about it?" she said.

Jane had the dazed air of someone who was in shock.

"Oh, Lizzy! I never thought anyone could be so happy!"

Thank heavens! If Bingley had proposed, then all would be well, and her dilemma would be resolved.

"Has he asked you—?" she said, eagerly.

"No. Not yet," said Jane, dreamily. "Lizzy, we almost – for a moment—." She stopped, crimson staining her cheeks. "— we almost kissed."

She said the words in a whisper.

Elizabeth's heart sank. Mr. Darcy and Elizabeth had kissed, and look at what happened with that. She could only conclude that young ladies always read more into such things than gentlemen.

"Did he make any suggestion—?" Elizabeth felt horrible for pressing Jane at a moment like this, but she needed to know if there was any chance that Darcy was wrong about Bingley's intentions.

"Lizzy, I know that he loves me. I am certain of it." She hugged herself. "He would have kissed me, if I had given him half a chance."

Like Darcy kissed Elizabeth? The memory of that brief contact – the velvet pressure of his lips against hers – was branded onto her skin.

She pushed the memory away. It meant nothing.

The same was true of Bingley who would have ridden away without the smallest hesitation. It was such a typical story. A fashionable young London gentleman captures the heart of an innocent country lady, entertaining himself at her expense, then decamping when he grows tired of the limited local society.

He is planning to leave and never come back, she wanted to say, but the joy on her sister's face stopped her. Elizabeth could not blot the radiance from Jane's face. If Mr. Bingley was leaving, Jane would find out soon enough.

What a dreadful thing love is, thought Elizabeth, and she hoped fervently that she would never see Mr. Darcy again.

∞ ∞ ∞

After leaving the walking party at Longbourn, Darcy and Bingley parted ways. Darcy claimed he needed to walk into the village for an errand, while Bingley looked like he was floating on a cloud.

He will fall down to earth with a thud very soon.

Darcy envied him his innocence, and he was not prepared to destroy it just yet. He would give him the chance to build castles in the sky for a few more hours. Darcy was in no hurry to take on the onerous task of disillusioning him.

Meanwhile, he did not know what to do himself. He wandered around aimlessly, his thoughts formless and turbulent, hardly aware of his surroundings. When he came to himself, he found himself standing at the gates to Longbourn.

He turned away, impatient and angry with himself, and walked towards Netherfield, feeling numb both inside and out, the cold nipping at his nose and ears. He raised his collar and huddled his shoulders under his great coat. His thin gloves were no match for the elements. His fingers were fast losing sensation.

No sense in getting frostbite wandering around the countryside when the fires would be roaring in Netherfield. In the end he returned to the house, defeated by the cold.

The moment he arrived at Netherfield, Miss Bingley appeared in the hallway. She must have been watching for him through the parlor window. He peeled off his gloves and tossed them down next to his hat.

"My brother tells me you have been wandering around quite aimlessly. You must come and sit by the fire and warm yourself."

Darcy did not need the invitation. He made his way to the closest fireplace to warm himself.

"Charles says Mrs. Bennet has improved a great deal."

Mrs. Bennet has not *improved,* he thought wildly. She had never been afflicted in the first place. He ground his teeth against the anger and the hurt, struggling to keep his expression neutral.

"Mrs. Bennet is in good health, and Mr. Bennet has returned to take care of his family." he replied. "We now have the carriage back, and I will be setting out for Town at dawn. I will have Evans pack my things."

"Shall we all start planning for our departure, then? I have a whole household to pack, and I would like to start issuing orders."

"As for when you are leaving, I suppose you must ask your brother. After all, he is master here at Netherfield."

Miss Bingley looked nonplussed at Darcy's unexpected characterization of Bingley.

"Yes, but—"

"We will discuss this later. I have an urgent letter to write."

It was a dishonest statement. That was how these things began, with a single precarious moment when the distinction between truth and deceit was hanging in the balance.

Taking the stairs two at time, Darcy retreated strategically to his bedchamber. From the bottom of the stairs, he heard Miss Bingley's voice calling his name, but he ignored it. In this grim mood, he was not completely in control. He might say something cutting to her. Or even worse, he might reveal the whole sorry business. *That* would give her a weapon to use, and he had no doubt Miss Bingley would brandish it to convince Bingley to depart at once. Darcy had not yet decided what to say to Bingley, and he did not want his sisters using Elizabeth's confession for their own purposes.

He rang loudly and repeatedly for Evans, who

arrived breathless and in record time.

"You rang for me, sir?"

No, I did not. You imagined it. Darcy bit down on the sarcastic reply. It was not his habit to take out his anger on the servants.

"We will be departing at dawn," he said. The words had a finality to them that threw him into despondency. "Do what should be done to make us ready."

"Yes, sir."

Evans disappeared briefly and returned with two footmen carrying Darcy's portmanteau and bags, and set about quietly going about his business.

Meanwhile, to avoid sliding down the slippery slope of duplicity—and to distract himself from the whirlwind of emotions battering at him—he forced himself to write a letter to his sister Georgiana. It was indeed urgent, so he had not lied to Miss Bingley. Distracted by his conundrum with Elizabeth Bennet, he had neglected poor Georgiana terribly.

It was impossible to concentrate, however, with all the activity going on in the room. Instead, he stared through the window across the open fields in the direction of Longbourn. Three miles away, Elizabeth Bennet was going about her everyday activities. He wondered if she was thinking about his departure, or if she was recounting their conversation, laughing at him with her sisters.

He gave a loud groan.

"Mr. Darcy. Are you in pain?"

How could he explain the groan?

"A wrong move. I jolted my shoulder," he said, and was annoyed at himself again for resorting to subterfuge.

"I will ask the housekeeper for something to ease the pain."

"No need," said Darcy. "I would prefer you to finish your packing."

He continued to stare out of the window, trying his best not to think of the hurt on Elizabeth's face before she walked away, until Evans completed his arrangements in the bedchamber, and the footmen carried down Darcy's baggage.

"I will fetch you some laudanum, shall I, sir?"

Darcy considered the possibility. Laudanum would give him the bliss of sleep and oblivion. It was tempting, but he preferred not to follow that path. Better to be consumed by desire for Elizabeth than to be consumed with desire for the tincture.

"Thank you, Evans. That will be all."

When his valet was gone, Darcy set aside his torment, throwing all his energy into writing the letter. It was a battle, and he struggled to keep his lines even. He had to redo the letter after the ink dripped from the quill onto the page when his mind drifted to the events of the last few hours. As he copied the whole page over, his hand felt heavy, and his handwriting was labored, slanting backwards then forwards in tangled mess. He laughed ironically. Miss

Bingley would not compliment him on his penmanship if she saw this letter. He remembered Elizabeth Bennet's amusement at Miss Bingley's fawning praise and his throat tightened painfully.

He would never see that laughter on Elizabeth's face again.

He imagined her leaning over his shoulder to survey the letter, as she and Miss Bingley had done on that day in the library. His breath quickened and his spine tingled at the idea of her standing close to him. He imagined her putting her arms around him and leaning against him as he sat in the chair. She would whisper in his ear, her warm breath caressing his skin and setting it on fire.

Enough! He refused to think of her.

Then he sealed the letter resolutely, satisfied that he had proved himself not to be a liar. If he sent this, Georgiana would probably discern his state of mind and set out at once to see him, but most likely, he would arrive before the letter.

Now he had one last task to accomplish – he needed to tell Bingley what had happened.

Chapter 9

Darcy did not leave Netherfield at dawn, nor did he tell Bingley the truth. He tried, in all honesty, but Bingley was in such high spirits Darcy did not have the heart to go through with it. Postponing his journey was not a good solution, obviously, but last night, when he did have an opportunity to speak to Bingley, Darcy had been too drained to deal with the situation, and he let it go.

He awoke, however, full of resolution. It was unconscionable to leave without ensuring Bingley had all the facts in his possession. Darcy owed it to his friend. Once he had told him, Bingley would be free to act on the information as he chose.

Darcy went down to breakfast early, anxious to get the whole business over and done with, but Bingley did not oblige him by appearing for breakfast. Darcy retreated to the library, leaving instructions with the butler, Mr. Stead, for Bingley to be awakened and informed that Darcy wished to speak to him there.

It was almost noon when Bingley finally strode into the library. Darcy was on the verge of giving up and setting out for London, his patience wearing thin.

"Ah, you are finally awake!" said Darcy, his voice censorious. "I thought you were going to wave me off this morning when I left."

"Sorry to disappoint, Darcy, but I need my sleep. Besides, since when do I rise at the crack of dawn to bid you farewell? That is more Caroline's domain than mine. Though if I had known you would take it so much to heart, I might have made the effort."

"Very funny," said Darcy.

"I thought so," said Bingley, sitting casually on the edge of the desk.

Bingley's cheerful mood grated on Darcy's nerves, not least because he himself felt as grumpy as a bear that was tied and being bated.

If you knew the truth, Bingley, you would not be quite that cheerful.

"Come on, Darcy. It's a beautiful day. Don't you fancy a quick gallop across the fields?"

The last thing he wanted was to go back to the fields that had landed them where they were now in the first place. If they had not encountered Collins that day, Darcy would never have discovered the lengths to which the Bennets were prepared to go to capture a husband. He would have departed with a memory of Elizabeth as he believed her to be – a model of honesty and candor in a corrupt world. Now he was left with nothing. His memories would be forever tainted.

As Bingley began to whistle a song Darcy recognized as a love ballad Miss Bingley liked to sing. Darcy's frustration doubled.

"Will you cease that confounded racket?"

Bingley stared at his friend. "What has gotten into you, Darcy? You have woken up with a sore head. Too much brandy last night?"

"After one sifter?" said Darcy. "Not very likely. I have a perfect right to object if you are whistling abysmally out of tune."

"I am not out of tune, Darcy. At least, I do not think so. And I am entitled to whistle out of tune in my own house, surely? Anyway, what did you wish to talk about that was so urgent?"

Bingley was so damnably cheerful, Darcy felt apprehensive breaking the bad news to him.

"I think you should leave this afternoon. Ride to London with me," said Darcy. "You need to get a different perspective."

"I should have known you would be harping on that same issue. It is growing tiresome. I have already had more than an earful from Caroline and Louisa. You are becoming a bore, you know."

"Because everyone is looking out for your interest." If he could convince Bingley to leave without revealing what had happened, he would much prefer it. "What harm can it do to leave for London with me

127

today? You can always come back if you feel strongly about it."

"But why today, in heaven's name? I have known you for years and I have never seen you give in to impulse. I am usually the one who does things in a ripping hurry. It is not like you to act on a whim."

"I beg your pardon, but I am far from acting on a whim. I seem to recall having a similar conversation a few days ago."

"Yes, but you did *not* depart then, which is yet another instance of your helter-skelter behavior. You usually stick to your decisions."

"As you know very well, Bingley, circumstances intervened. The Miss Bennets were in a tenuous situation."

Or so he had believed.

"Yes, I understand that, but then you stayed beyond that first day. Why did you do that? *You* do not care about the Bennets."

Bingley mulled over this, then suddenly brightened and slapped Darcy on the back.

"Unless you do! Of course! You are a *sly* one, Darcy, but I have ferreted out your secret. You really care for Miss Elizabeth. Caroline has been teasing you about it for some time, and I knew you were attracted to her, but I did not think it *that* serious. But what if it is?" He observed Darcy keenly. "Well, is it?"

Darcy frowned. Any confession of his interest in Elizabeth would be the kiss of death to his plans of departure. Bingley would hound him mercilessly, eager to exploit his weakness to keep him in Meryton.

It was time to strip Bingley of his illusions.

"If I did, I would not be fool enough to tell you, Bingley. Besides, that is not why I wanted to talk to you."

"Aha! I knew something was up." The delighted expression on Bingley's face told Darcy he was still harping on the matter of Elizabeth Bennet.

"I have something *unpleasant* to discuss. I hope we will not be interrupted. I am sorry to say—"

There was a scratch at the door and Bingley responded without thinking. "Come in."

"Mr. Bennet is here, sir," intoned Mr. Stead.

"Mr. Bennet?" Bingley slid from the desk with an eager expression. "Bring him here immediately."

Darcy groaned. "I *had* hoped we would not be interrupted."

But Bingley had other concerns now.

"I hope he is not here to ask me about my intentions towards Miss Bennet."

Darcy stood up and walked to the window.

"More likely, he is here to issue an invitation, now that he is here."

"I dearly hope so," said Bingley, eagerly. "Although it could be something else. I hope Mrs. Bennet has not suffered a relapse."

Darcy knew only too well how impossible that

was. He kept silent. He would come to that matter soon enough.

The door opened and the footman announced Mr. Bennet.

"Mr. Bennet! How delightful to see you," said Bingley, bowing and smiling effusively at the older gentleman.

"Thank you. I hope you are well, Mr. Bingley."

"Perfectly well, sir. And you?"

"Very well indeed."

Mr. Bennet looked towards Darcy. "I wonder if I might speak privately to you, Mr. Darcy. It is a matter of some delicacy."

Darcy started. He could not imagine what Mr. Bennet had to say to him.

With a bow, Darcy indicated the leather armchair. "Of course."

Bingley cleared his throat. "Yes, well, I shall leave you to it, then, shall I?"

Mr. Bennet inclined his head with an amused quirk of his brow and took the offered seat, waiting for Mr. Bingley to leave before speaking. Bingley left slowly, obviously hoping he would be called back.

Meanwhile, Darcy was consumed with impatience, wondering what mysterious errand had brought Mr. Bennet to Netherfield. Did it have something to do with Elizabeth? Had she complained that he had insulted her? If that was the case, too bad. He would not apologize. *He* was the one who was wronged.

"No doubt you have guessed my purpose in calling on you. I have come to offer an apology on behalf of my wife. Lizzy has informed me of the substance of your conversation. I can only suppose that you feel wronged."

Darcy was taken aback. It felt uncanny for Mr. Bennet to echo what he was thinking, and it threw him off balance. The sense of righteous indignation that had fueled him since yesterday dissipated suddenly into thin air, making him feel hollow.

It was handsome of Mr. Bennet to apologize, but Darcy could not simply accept the apology and behave as if nothing had happened. Yet he could not voice his accusations, either. What did one say in such a situation?

I no longer trust Elizabeth. It breaks my heart, but she has lost my good opinion, and I do not see how she could ever recover it. I feel as though my life is in ruins.

He could not say anything like that.

"I believed Mrs. Bennet to be in imminent danger. I believed it to be an emergency. I was concerned about her health. I even sent for you. Then I discovered it was little more than a hoax."

Darcy had wanted to sound angry and disappointed, but his sense of betrayal must have been stronger than either of those, because the words sounded aggrieved.

The amusement vanished from Mr. Bennet's expression. He sighed heavily.

"I know. It was unforgivable. I understand your indignation only too well, Mr. Darcy. I felt it myself."

Mr. Bennet steepled his hands and studied Darcy gravely. Darcy fidgeted, feeling as if Mr. Bennet could see right through him. An unexpected notion came to him. If he—by some unlikely chance—were to marry Elizabeth, this gentleman would be his father.

"It was not my wife's intent to deceive you," said Mr. Bennet. "You were not supposed to know about it. Mrs. Bennet simply wanted to fool Mr. Collins—a gentleman who, I am sure you will agree, is very easily fooled. Her intent was to return to full health as soon as he came back from his errand. It was simply an accident of fate that you came to learn that she was indisposed. I am sure when you were in Oxford you engaged in one or two pranks of your own. Think of this as a prank that went awry."

Darcy found it difficult to perceive the whole situation as nothing more than a prank. There had been too much said and done for him to regard it so trivially.

Mr. Bennet must have understood again what was on his mind, because he made a dismissive gesture.

"Anyway, enough said. When you have given it some more consideration, you may look at it differently. That was not my main purpose in speaking to you." Mr. Bennet paused. "You will have to tell me how much I owe you. I would like to repay what you spent dispatching the carriage for my return."

"From what I gathered, sir, it was my own folly that incurred the expense and the inconvenience—for you—of an early return. Miss Elizabeth did her best to talk me out of it, but I did not pay her heed. If anything, please allow me to offer my coach so you can return to the side of your friend."

"I thank you, sir, for your generous offer." Mr. Bennet fell silent. "Unfortunately, an express arrived this morning to inform me that my friend has passed away."

The full folly of his own actions struck Darcy forcibly. By not listening to Elizabeth, he had deprived Mr. Bennet of the chance to spend his last hours with a dying friend.

"I am truly sorry to hear it." He was overwhelmed by dejection. He had caused so much harm even when he intended to do good. "If you are planning to attend the funeral, sir, my carriage is at your disposal. It does not make up for the precious hours you lost, but at least you may travel to the funeral in comfort."

It was inadequate. Darcy was dismayed at the inconvenience he had incurred by forcing Mr. Bennet to travel back again.

Mr. Bennet rose to his feet. "Thank you. I may well take you up on your offer. Meanwhile, I also had another purpose in calling. I was hoping you will accept an invitation to shoot tomorrow."

Darcy could not very well refuse under the circumstances. Besides, his departure had once again been thwarted. He could not travel to London and send the carriage back before the funeral. He would have to wait.

In any case, he was beginning to see his own behavior in a different light. Mr. Bennet had given him another way of looking at the whole sorry situation. And his own involvement in it had made everything worse. He had been so determined to form a good impression, he had disregarded Elizabeth's objections. If he had listened to Elizabeth, he would have waited before sending the carriage for Mr. Bennet.

He did not feel any more charitable towards Mrs. Bennet, nor did he approve of her plan to marry Miss Lydia to the reprehensible Collins. But he could not blame Elizabeth for what was mostly a series of unfortunate events.

"I would be happy to do so, Mr. Bennet."

"Good. Then I will see you early tomorrow."

Darcy nodded, and with a quick bow, Mr. Bennet left.

"I see Mr. Bennet is gone," said Bingley, wandering in and looking glum. "What could he possibly have said to you in confidence? I hope he was not here to discourage me from courting Miss Bennet."

"Nothing like that," said Darcy. "He came to consult me on a financial matter."

Which was at least partially true; he did not

need to dissemble.

"Thank heavens!" Bingley went to the window to watch Mr. Bennet ride away. "I wish I had known. I have been pacing the picture gallery in torment this past half-hour."

"Mr. Bennet would not be so indiscrete as to approach me on a private matter that concerns you. I am not your brother or father, you know."

Bingley thought about this for a moment. "I suppose not, but the devil take it! I think of nothing but Miss Bennet all day. There are cobwebs in my brain."

"Well, that can be remedied easily enough. Mr. Bennet has invited us to shoot pheasants tomorrow. That should clear the cobwebs."

"Excellent news!" said Mr. Bingley. "Why did you not say so earlier? We will have a perfect excuse to call on the Bennet sisters." He cast a doubtful look towards Darcy. "Unless you are still determined to leave for Town?"

"I have promised Mr. Bennet my carriage to attend a funeral. I must wait for him to return."

Mr. Bingley chortled and clapped Darcy on the back. "How very convenient!"

"What do you mean?" Darcy frowned.

"Nothing, old fellow. Nothing at all."

Darcy was too preoccupied with Mr. Bennet to attend to Bingley's words. He was not sure what to make of Mr. Bennet's visit. It was the first time he had spoken to Elizabeth's father in private, and he was surprised to find Mr. Bennet more perceptive than he expected. Darcy also appreciated Mr. Bennet's offer to repay the carriage expenses. It showed he was an honorable man with a strong sense of obligation.

As for Mr. Bennet's apology for his wife's behavior—.

A sudden idea struck Darcy with the blinding effect of a lightning bolt. It was astounding it had not occurred to him earlier.

Rather than despising Mrs. Bennet for interrupting Mr. Collins' proposal, Darcy should in fact feel indebted to her. Were it not for Mrs. Bennet, Elizabeth would now be engaged to Mr. Collins.

He struck his brow with the flat of his hand.

"What is it, Darcy?" said Bingley, with alarm.

"Nothing. Only that sometimes I am not as clever as I imagined."

Bingley grinned. "I am very pleased to see you acknowledge it at long last."

Chapter 10

It was raining heavily in the morning and there was no chance of going shooting with Mr. Bennet. Darcy was surprised at the deep sense of disappointment he experienced. He had hoped at least to encounter Elizabeth, even if he did not know how matters could be mended between them.

Left without purpose, he did not join the others downstairs; he was in no mood for company. He fetched himself a book from the library, and endeavored to read it, without much success. He wrote another letter to Georgiana, although he had not yet heard back from her.

Somehow, the grey, heavy day passed.

By the time the rain stopped, and the clouds came out, the afternoon was well advanced, and the pheasants had already settled in the hedges and it was too late to ride over to Longbourn.

He was brought out of his room by a great commotion and a slamming of doors. Surprised and reluctant to be involved, he hovered at the top of the stairs to see if he was needed. The front door was open, and Caroline Bingley was shouting after her brother.

"Come back here at once, Charles!" said Miss Bingley. "You will rue the day you did this! Do not do anything hasty! We will discuss it further!"

She spotted Darcy at the top of the stairs and called out to him.

"Oh, Mr. Darcy!. You will never guess what my foolish brother intends to do! He says he is riding to Longbourn to propose to Jane Bennet."

She burst into tears.

Tears made him nervous, but he could not very well turn and go back to his room, so he came down the stairs to see if he could at least stop Bingley from leaving. He looked out and found Bingley setting off down the driveway.

"Mr. Bennet invited us to shoot with him," said Darcy, trying to placate Miss Bingley, though he knew it was unlikely. "I shall be heading in that direction myself."

"I do not believe that for an instant, Mr. Darcy. Charles said very clearly that he was going to ask for her hand, and that we should not expect him for dinner."

Well. Darcy had not expected that.

"He might have said that to annoy you, because he is tired of being told what to do and what not to do," he suggested.

It was a sentiment Darcy could relate to. He

himself was heartily sick of the threats that had been drilled into him, and the dire warnings of ancestors turning in their graves. Why must some long-dead predecessor have a say in his life?

"I wish you would not discount the possibility, Mr. Darcy. Charles said he had to go now because he wants to speak to Mr. Bennet before he journeys to Gloucestershire." She grasped the corner of his sleeve. "You cannot allow it. You must go after him at once and stop him before he ruins us all."

A week ago, he would have done so, but now he felt it was a losing battle. Darcy had stayed up most of the night pondering Mr. Bennet's words. He no longer considered Miss Bennet or Elizabeth complicit in their mother's scheming. While he could not yet regard what Mrs. Bennet did as a harmless prank, he was very glad she had intervened. The very thought of Collins marrying Elizabeth made Darcy's stomach curdle. Mrs. Bennet had put a stop to a marriage that could have brought nothing but misery to both parties.

Happiness in marriage was not something discussed very often in the upper echelons of society. In the feudal times, marriages were alliances intended as a means of consolidating power. He understood that. The Darcys had maintained their position since the Norman Conquest because they had chosen these alliances wisely. But was that the only way to do it? Through marrying someone who would never be anything but a stranger?

Surely happiness should be a consideration between people who intended to share a lifetime together.

Fortunately for Bingley -- unlike Darcy -- he did not have ancestors who would haunt him if he diminished the Darcy fortunes. Bingley might well improve his standing if he married a lady who was highly placed in society, but it would be a cold, mercenary marriage. Was it fair to expect Bingley to throw away a chance to find joy in his life?

"I will go after him, Miss Bingley, but I will not prevent him if he is really determined to take this step. I do believe Miss Bennet will make your brother happy."

Miss Bingley shook her head angrily.

"I do not know how the Bennets managed to have you both in their thrall. I wish we had never come to Meryton. It has been nothing but a disaster. Do you realize that I have no prospect now of finding a husband who is well placed in society?"

"I do not know if that is the case, Miss Bingley. I am sure your sister can introduce you to one of Mr. Hurst's acquaintances, though I do hope he might be a little more animated than her own husband."

"A lady cannot always choose. Time is not on our side."

It must be difficult to be a woman, he reflected, knowing her fate depended on securing a husband.

"I am not unsympathetic, Miss Bingley, but I cannot change the rules of society. If Bingley has the chance to find someone who will enrich his life, then I wish him well."

∞ ∞ ∞

Darcy went after Bingley as quickly as he could, considering he had to wait for his horse to be saddled. Such was Bingley's haste in riding to Longbourn, Darcy had a hard time catching up with him. By the time he did, they were almost there.

"If you have come to talk me out of it, Darcy, you may as well save your breath. Caroline has already made my head hurt with her long list of reasons I cannot marry Miss Bennet. But those reasons mean nothing to me. I love her, Darcy, and that is all that matters. You cannot stop me."

"I have not come to stop you, Bingley. I have come to give my support."

Bingley reined in and stared at him in astonishment.

"Good heavens, Darcy. I never thought I would hear you say such a thing. I almost broke my neck trying to get away from you."

"I am not your keeper, you know," said Darcy. "Tell me, if I had forbidden you from doing it, would that have prevented you?"

Bingley grinned. "Honestly? No. I would have stood my ground. But I would far rather have your blessing."

"I do not think you need it, but for what it is worth, you have it."

Bingley looked delighted and gave him a vigorous slap on the back, almost knocking Darcy sideways.

"I always knew you were a good friend."

Darcy really hoped he *was* being a good friend by encouraging Bingley to marry into the Bennet family. It would certainly not improve his social status. It was up to Miss Bingley now to elevate their family position.

"Since you are absolutely determined to ruin yourself, I have little choice in the matter," said Darcy ruefully. "Have you given a thought to what you are planning to say? Perhaps I can help you rehearse your speech."

"Rehearse my speech?" said Bingley, looking appalled. "Surely not! I cannot ask Jane – Miss Bennet – to marry me by rote! I will simply go on my knee, declare my love, and humbly beg her to marry me."

Darcy could not imagine that he would ever be able to propose to any young lady without preparing a speech.

Bingley's fate was sealed within less than half an hour. A quick visit to Mr. Bennet in the library brought Bingley out beaming. He and Jane Bennet then went out to the garden, leaving everyone waiting with bated breath.

Meanwhile, Darcy was left feeling like a spare thumb. No one paid him much attention, and his polite attempts to converse with Elizabeth were met with quick replies that made it clear she had not reconsidered her opinion of him.

He fought against dejection, but it was for the best. There would be no way of repairing the damage now. Perhaps he should go to London on horseback. It would be a long, cold ride, but he would survive it.

He was standing near one of the corner windows. It gave him a view over the garden just as Bingley and Miss Bennet emerged from behind a wall.

He saw Miss Bennet lifting her face to Bingley's in a kind of wonder, her expression that of a woman transfixed by a powerful emotion. The serene prettiness was gone, replaced by a feeling so profound he felt something shift inside him. He could not see Bingley's face, but there was reverence in every inch of his friend's body. They were murmuring to each other. Bingley bent towards Miss Bennet, and for a moment Darcy was convinced he would kiss her, but she shook her head, and with a gentle smile, stepped back out of his reach. There was no mistaking the love that shone in her eyes, even at this distance.

He had been wrong all along. There was no plot here, no nefarious plan to entrap Bingley. There was no longer any question in his mind that Miss Bennet was as much in love with Darcy's friend as Bingley was in love with her.

Darcy withdrew as quietly as he could, ashamed of witnessing such an intimate moment, shaken to the core.

In that moment he knew he would give away all his fortune to see love like that shining in Elizabeth's eyes.

∞∞∞

News of the engagement was received as loudly and jubilantly as Darcy would have anticipated. Everyone expressed their delight in the prospect. Mrs. Bennet talked to Mr. Bingley of nothing else but the engagement and the wedding. Miss Bennet glowed, and Bingley beamed, and everyone made merry.

As darkness fell, it was to be expected that the gentlemen would be invited to dine with them.

"You must stay for dinner, Mr. Bingley. Now that you are part of the family, we need not stand on any ceremony."

Mrs. Bennet darted a look in his direction. It was not difficult to read. This was to be a celebration of sorts, and he was not invited. He could stay, of course. They would not turn him away if he decided to join them. He looked towards Elizabeth, trying to deter-mine whether he would be welcome. One glance from her, he thought. That was all he needed. A glance, or a sign, and he would stay.

But she was looking away. He could not catch her eye. She was all smiles, and her pleasure at her sister's engagement was apparent, but he was forgotten.

He had no reason to stay.

"If I might take my leave," he said. "I am expected for dinner at Netherfield."

"Oh, Mr. Darcy," said Jane. "You *must* stay for dinner. I am sure Charles—" she blushed furiously as she said Bingley's name, "—Charles would wish you to join us."

"Well, of course, any friend of Mr. Bingley's is welcome, I am sure," said Mrs. Bennet, stiffly.

And so it was decided. If it were not for Bingley's obvious jubilation, he would have turned away and returned to Netherfield to lick his wounds, but for his friend's sake he resigned himself for an evening that could bring him only misery.

The dinner was a torment. No other word could describe it. His original impression that Elizabeth was giving him the cold shoulder was confirmed as she studiously avoided looking at him. Mrs. Bennet was full of joyous exclamations, and her conversation revolved around marriage settlements, dates, and trips to London to visit the modiste and measure for wedding clothes. Darcy felt like a starving waif looking through a window at a dining table full of food. He could observe, but he could not touch, and he felt consumed with bitterness at being left out of this merry party.

Darcy was intensely relieved when the covers were removed, and the ladies sauntered out of the room, leaving the four gentlemen to their brandy and cigars.

Darcy watched Elizabeth go wistfully. He had not had a chance to speak to her privately all evening. She was too absorbed in her sister's happiness to heed him, or worse, she was deliberately ignoring him.

Unlike him, she had not forgotten their quarrel. While he had been able to forgive and forget, it was clear that she did not feel the same. He remembered his words that day at Netherfield in the library, when he had pronounced – sounding like an utterly pompous fool – that his good opinion, once lost, was lost forever. What if Elizabeth was inclined to hold a grudge? A cold chill settled into his very soul. Would he ever obtain her forgiveness for misjudging her?

He was gripped by the urgent need to stalk over to her and throw himself at her mercy.

"I am looking forward to seeing you at Rosings -- my esteemed patronesses' house -- particularly after a certain happy event takes place," said Mr. Collins, sending a significant look towards Mr. Bennet. "It will all feel very familiar, since we have been thrown into each other's company so often."

Mr. Bennet looked bemused, while Bingley looked puzzled. Had Lydia succeeded in capturing Mr. Collins' attention after all?

"And what event may that be?" said Darcy, curious to discover the outcome of Mrs. Bennet's stratagems.

"Why, my marriage to Cousin Elizabeth."

The air was squeezed from Darcy's lungs. He gripped the edge of the table to steady himself. He felt as if the ground had moved beneath him.

"Mr. Darcy," said Mr. Bennet. "Are you unwell?"

Darcy fought to emerge from the sensation that his ribs were being crushed. He took a shuddering breath. Everyone was looking at him. He could not allow them to guess the reason for his reaction.

"A sudden spasm," said Darcy, forcing his voice to be calm. "It will pass, I am sure."

Another deception. When would all this end? Another untruth added to the others.

He rose to his feet shakily. "If you will point me in the direction of the outhouse? I hope you will excuse me a moment."

It was humiliating to use such a vulgar excuse, but he needed air. He needed to think.

Mr. Bennet hastened to give him directions, while Mr. Collins blathered on – something about a tincture Lady Catherine had recommended to him for just these kinds of situations.

Darcy did not go to the outhouse, but he went *out*. He could not stand to be indoors with the walls closing in on him. It was a bitterly cold night, with a clear, crisp sky dotted with stars and a white moon that spread its cold light over everything. It was December already, Darcy thought, and observed in a curiously detached way that there would be frost by morning.

The cold gave him the kick in the teeth he needed, and he began to breathe again, each breath forming a cloud before dispersing. It was strange to be wandering about on the grounds of Longbourn in the dark alone like this. His footsteps crushed the gravel under his feet, sounding loud in the still winter night.

This was her territory, he thought, Elizabeth's. Her footsteps as a child must have taken this path very often, running, skipping rope, chasing her sisters. He was certain she would have climbed these trees and fallen from these branches.

There was a swing tied to a thick branch of an old oak tree. He went and sat on it, twisting the rope, and twirling it back and forth. He could imagine Elizabeth doing the same, perhaps holding a book in one hand.

He sat in the swing, where he imagined she liked to sit, and let the torment wash over him.

Elizabeth was about to marry Collins. Collins had proposed while Darcy had been busy nursing his pride and licking his wounds and trying to decide what to do. She had agreed to marry her cousin because she believed Darcy to be leaving and never coming back.

She was to marry Collins. The horrible truth sank in.

He tried not to imagine Elizabeth in Mr. Collins' arms. The idea disgusted him so much his stomach revolted. To think of that man's thick clumsy hands touching her body—

It was not to be borne. How would she endure such a man, day after day? He could not be in the same room with that toady for more than a few minutes, let alone be stuck with him for a lifetime.

But what could he do?

There was a rock in Darcy's stomach. A huge boulder with sharp edges that jabbed into him and caused agonizing pain. The very thought of that despicable little man stealing away Elizabeth from him, his thick fingers touching Elizabeth's body made Darcy ill.

To make matters worse, Darcy would have to see them together whenever he went to visit Lady Catherine. He would have to be polite to her and endure the sight of her bearing the loathsome man's children.

Something began to niggle at Darcy, and he sat up straight, his mind racing.

Why had there been no mention of the engagement earlier? No talk of a double wedding during dinner? No blushing on Elizabeth's part and no exclamations from Mrs. Bennet? Even if Elizabeth's mother was disappointed that Collins was not marrying Lydia, surely she would have been eager to mention that another of her daughters was getting married.

He pondered this for several minutes, swinging back and forth, the branch creaking rhythmically under his weight.

If anyone was to marry her, it would have to be him. Fitzwilliam Darcy, of Pemberley, Derbyshire.

No announcement had been made. There was still a chance.

He would have to find Elizabeth and talk to her.

Chapter 11

"You are sitting in my swing, Mr. Darcy."

He was startled when a shadow detached itself from the trunk of another tree and appeared before him. Even if she had not spoken, her outline against the light inside the house was unmistakable.

He stepped down from the swing at once. He could not afford to offend her, not when nothing had been resolved between them, and this one was a very easy thing to resolve.

"I did not mean to take your place," he said.

He sounded stiff and awkward, insecure about his reception. He had everything to lose if Elizabeth refused to talk to him.

To his relief, she did not go away. She sat on the swing he had vacated. Unlike him, he noticed, she kept her feet firmly on the ground and sat motionless.

They were alone. He had not expected to meet her here. He was both thrilled and terrified it had happened. He plunged ahead, reckless and impatient, unable to endure his uncertainty a moment longer.

"May I have a word with you, Miss Elizabeth?" Darcy broke into her thoughts.

"If a word with me means you plan to chide me and accuse me of nefarious dealings, then perhaps it would be better to indulge in small-talk. I do not wish to take up where we left off." She paused. "I believe it is customary to talk about the weather. It is certainly the safest topic for us to discuss."

"I would rather not discuss the weather, Miss Elizabeth. I have other matters I wish to pursue."

"Very well, Mr. Darcy. You can start by explaining why you are in the garden instead of drinking brandy with the gentlemen."

"I am here because I am avoiding your cousin."

He watched for any indication that the engagement had taken place, but she did not react. Nor did she correct him and say Collins was her fiancé.

There was really no point in talking about anything else if she was engaged. It was embarrassing, but he needed to know the answer too desperately not to approach it directly.

"He referred to the possibility of an engagement."

"Mr. Collins?"

"Yes."

"It is already settled, you know."

Darcy's heart dropped. It was too late. He ought to have offered for her before. If he had not been so wrapped up in his own sense of aggrievement, if he had not been feeling so sorry for himself, then he could have prevented it.

"I see," he said. 'Then I take it congratulations are in order."

"Congratulations? Oh. You misunderstand me. When I said settled, I meant that I would not accept Mr. Collins under any condition. Mama would consider it an insult if I took him away from Lydia, and Papa has indicated he will never talk to me if I marry him, so you see I could never say yes. Not that I ever considered doing it. I would have refused him in the first place, if I had not been interrupted."

She laughed softly.

"So you see, this whole muddle with Mama was completely unnecessary. She did not need to interrupt me, because I would have refused him anyway."

Relief made him giddy. He wanted to pick her up and spin around with her and laugh. This was excellent news.

Why had he never considered that possibility? Yet again, he had not given Miss Elizabeth enough credit for knowing her own mind.

At last, he had an opportunity to clear the air. He did not deceive himself that it would be easy. It was quite possible that they would quarrel again. He cringed at the prospect of regurgitating their whole argument. He had no idea how it would end, but it had to be done.

At least he had a very good sense of where he should start.

"I would like to offer you an apology."

"So you *do* intend to continue where we left off," she said. "I wish you would spare both of us the unpleasantness."

He felt much the same, but there was too much at stake.

"First an apology, then an explanation," he said, earnestly. "If we each explain our point of view, we might be able to understand each other. Do you agree?"

He wished there was more light, so he could read her expression.

"I suppose so," she said, with obvious reluctance.

"Since I became master at Pemberley, I have been approached by all manner of fortune-hunting young ladies, their mothers in tow, words of flattery dripping from their lips. Over the years, I have come to despise pretension of any kind, and have become particularly sensitive to any attempts to trick or entice me into situations that might force my hand."

Elizabeth pursed her lips and threw him an angry look.

"I was expecting an apology, Mr. Darcy, not a speech about your social importance. While I understand your position perfectly, Mr. Darcy, I can assure you that none of us had any intention whatsoever of forcing your hand. If anything, Mama has done everything she can to discourage you from approaching us. I hope you will acknowledge the truth of that. Have you ever seen any sign from any of us that we wish to entrap you in any way?"

Mr. Darcy gave a brittle laugh.

"None whatsoever," he acceded. "But the explanation for that is very simple. Mrs. Bennet knew better than to waste her time on *me*. She has given her full attention to my friend Bingley instead, knowing that he is much more easily trapped than I am."

She made a sound of frustration in her throat.

"Is that it, then. Is that all the apology you have to offer?"

He felt bewildered. He was not in the habit of giving elaborate apologies. He did not know what she expected of him.

"I—"

She did not let him continue. "You have mistaken the situation completely. I should point out that Mama's reluctance does not come from considering that you are too far above us. Only *arrogance* can prompt you to think so. I regard you as my equal. You are a gentleman; I am a gentleman's daughter."

"I am aware of that, madam. But I do not understand how that is supposed to change my perception of Mrs. Bennet."

"If you throw your mind back to that first encounter we had, and recall the words you spoke, you will realize we have good reason to think you arrogant. Do you recall what you said? Something along the lines of a certain young lady not being *tolerable enough* to tempt you?"

Darcy started, recognizing the words.

"Did Bingley tell you?"

"Mr. Bingley did not need to tell me. You told me so yourself. You did not even trouble to lower your voice so I would not hear you."

He felt the blood rise to his face.

"You were not intended to hear it. I believed the noise of the ballroom would prevent the words from reaching you."

"You were looking straight at me when you said it. Even if I did not hear you, do you think I did not see the sneering expression that was obviously aimed at me?"

"I—" He could not find a way to excuse himself. He had not done it deliberately, but he *had* intended to put her in her place. He spread his hands in a gesture of – what? He was not quite sure. Possibly supplication.

"I am sorry for the distress I caused you," he said.

"I was not asking for an apology," she said, "though I do believe you. I am just giving you an explanation for Mama's attitude. A gentleman who snubbed her daughter in such an obvious manner could never be welcome. *That* is why she does not like you."

No one liked to hear that someone disliked them. It did not make him feel any better. He had to ignore the set-down and focus on what Elizabeth was telling him. It was certainly not what he expected. How many society ladies would easily forgive him a snub, if there was even a remote chance that he might single out their daughters?

Mrs. Bennet was not one of those women, apparently.

"Then your mother is a gem indeed," said Darcy, "if she is willing to discount the possibility of a match between us because of injured pride."

She nodded. There was something regal about the way she inclined her head, and he saw it now, when he had not noticed it at all before. Elizabeth was too *proud* to use subterfuge and to resort to tricks and stratagems. If a gentleman wanted to marry her, he would have to be eager, or not at all.

"You believe in love as a basis for marriage?"

"Is it so very strange that I would want the gentleman who is my husband to love me?"

The question hung in the air. It tugged at something deep inside him.

She twirled on the swing, twisting the rope until it was completely tight, then releasing it like a spring. She spun around, airy and graceful as a dancer.

She was unfettered, completely unconscious of her loveliness. His breath caught in his throat.

A wave of tenderness swept through him, cresting and frothing until it filled his whole being, washing away the last traces of his anger.

"No, not strange, given who you are," he said, softly.

But she was not yet finished with him. She still had a few knots to untangle before she would accept him. He prepared to listen, no longer driven to prove a point.

"I am sorry that your life is so blighted by matchmaking mamas, but may I remind you that the whole purpose of the London Season is precisely to match young ladies of good breeding to the highest bidder. What you are saying is true of all young gentlemen of a certain social standing. It is how society functions, Mr. Darcy. Do you think we do not deserve the same chance at securing a good marriage because we do not possess a fortune?"

She stopped. Was she railing against him, or against the world? He really did not know how to answer, or even if it was a question at all.

"As for Mr. Bingley, I would like to know who appointed you as his keeper? Have you ever considered that he might truly care for my sister, and that she might truly care for him?

"I have considered it," he said, quietly.

She gave a little laugh and jumped off the swing.

She still had not noticed that he was no longer arguing with her.

"Come, Mr. Darcy," she said, "we must return to the house, or someone will shout compromise at finding us unchaperoned in the dark. Let us agree to disagree. It is hard for us to see eye to eye on anything. Since we are unfortunate enough to be trapped together for several minutes, strolling the grounds, let us speak about something bland. I will leave it to you to choose the topic."

He gave her a faint smile. "I assure you, I do not feel unfortunate, nor trapped in the least."

"Ah, it was a bad choice of words on my part, was it not? You will now take this as a confession that I have designs on your fortune."

"I will not do any such thing," he said. "You are deliberately misrepresenting me."

"Rest assured, Mr. Darcy, you are not in any danger from *me*. You are entirely safe in my hands."

Darcy's thoughts immediately turned in a distinctly uncomfortable direction as he looked down at Miss Elizabeth's long fingers, encased in soft kid gloves.

I assure you, I would feel entirely safe in your hands, he wanted to say, but of course he would not say that out loud.

"I am not afraid of you, Miss Elizabeth," he said, laughing at the irony of it all, "since I know that *you* of all people are not inclined to flatter me."

"Then it seems we are in agreement about something, after all," she said.

The hardness had left her voice. Her voice was light and teasing.

He could not make her out. Did she mean to tease him? Did she know he cared for her? Did she have any idea that she inhabited his thoughts day and night?

"We are more in agreement than you think," he said, since she still saw him as an enemy. "That is why I wanted to apologize."

When she made a sound of protest, he hurried on.

"I – made a hash of things earlier." He hesitated. It was not easy for him to admit he was wrong. His pride rebelled. But if he wanted to redeem himself with her, he had no choice but to be humble.

"Since we had our quarrel, I have come to see things differently. Let us say I witnessed something that changed my mind about your sister's affections. I do not believe her indifferent to my friend."

"I am heartily glad of that, at least. There is not a duplicitous bone in Jane's body. She is simply – reserved and serene."

He nodded. "I know that now. More importantly, I am happy for Bingley, and happy they are engaged." He was pleased to see her head jerk up in surprise. "As you so rightly stated, I am not my friend's keeper. If my friend is not concerned about marrying into a title or improving his social standing, then who am I to question it?"

"But you believe he could do better."

It was a challenge. He sensed that his reply was important to her. He considered the question carefully.

"Bingley's father worked hard to improve their social status. I know he would have wanted his children to foster good connections. It was why he sent Bingley to boarding school and then to Oxford. Bingley's leasing of Netherfield was intended to help establish him as a landed gentleman. Because of his wealth, there was a strong chance he could marry into a titled family that were short of funds." He shrugged. "He might have succeeded in both these aims. Or he might not. Who knows? I think the issue is that he seems to have chosen a different path, and I cannot fault him for choosing love over pragmatism."

Once again, Darcy felt an intense longing for a happiness he might never have. He stole a glance at Miss Elizabeth. Their eyes met.

I envy Bingley this opportunity, he wanted to say. *I dream of such happiness with you.*

His heart gave a little hop. Did she feel the same?

Then she looked away and the moment was gone. He did not pursue it. It was enough for him now that they had reconciled some of their differences. He did not want to push his luck.

But he parted with Elizabeth in a far better

frame of mind. Their conversation had taught him to hope.

Chapter 12

D arcy thought of nothing all night but the possibility of Collins offering for Elizabeth again. Although she had assured him she would not accept the clergyman, Darcy could not be easy until he knew Collins was no longer a candidate. Darcy was certain the Bennet household awoke early, and if there was any chance that Collins was going to renew his offer, Darcy was not about to risk it.

There was only one way to make sure that Collins failed in his objective, and that was for Darcy to propose to Elizabeth himself.

Fortunately, Darcy had a perfect excuse to call on the Bennets early the next morning. He was sending his carriage to pick up Mr. Bennet and take him back to Gloucestershire for the funeral. It was perfectly natural for Darcy to use the carriage to transport him and Bingley to Longbourn.

Wild horses would not keep Darcy away from Longbourn in any case.

Bingley was more than eager to join him. They

arrived as the family was sitting at breakfast. In any other situation, their arrival at this time would be an unforgivable lapse of decorum, but Bingley would always be welcome.

"I beg your pardon for intruding," said Darcy, bowing formally, "but since Mr. Bingley is now part of the family, I hope you do not mind that I joined him."

His gaze sought Elizabeth. She looked endearingly flustered at his sudden arrival, and his heart gave a little leap as he dared to hope.

"Mr. Bingley is always welcome, of course," said Mrs. Bennet, cutting Darcy out completely, and smiling at her future son. Bingley could do no wrong, especially now that he had declared himself.

There would have been a time when Darcy might have been affronted at being snubbed by Mrs. Bennet. Now that he knew the reason, he found it diverting that Mrs. Bennet did not make the slightest attempt to ingratiate herself to him. It confirmed what Elizabeth had said. Mrs. Bennet was not simply a grasping fortune hunter. She had made up her mind that she did not like Darcy, and that was enough reason for her to overlook his fortune completely.

Darcy exchanged glances with Elizabeth, and the merriment in her dark eyes found an echo inside him. He smiled at her – a wide open smile, and when she returned it, the very core of his being melted. He was lost forever in that smile.

He had tumbled headlong. He should be terrified, but it filled him with exhilaration.

What would it be like to encounter such a smile every morning for the rest of his life over breakfast? He would be blissfully happy.

The way her gaze settled on him suggested she might be prepared to accept the possibility.

"Would you like to sit down, Mr. Darcy?" said Mr. Bennet, jovially. "You may squeeze yourself in wherever you choose."

But it was Mrs. Bennet who took charge, pointing everyone to their seats. The arrangement was completely informal, dependent on Mrs. Bennet's whim. In another snub, no concession was made to Darcy's rank. Mr. and Mrs. Bennet were at the head of the table, Mr. Bingley was next to Mrs. Bennet, with Miss Bennet opposite him, and Elizabeth next to her father. Darcy, meanwhile, was positioned at the bottom of the table, further even than Collins, who was clearly regarded as more desirable than him. He found himself next to Mary, who was relegated to the end.

He should be glad, he supposed, that there was one person at the table who was considered by Mrs. Bennet to be lower than him.

There was a great deal of shuffling as chairs and plates were moved to accommodate the newcomers, accompanied by laughter as cups and silverware were left behind and had to be passed down. Collins managed to slosh some of his coffee onto the tablecloth, and Lydia took the opportunity to dab at his cravat with her napkin, leaning close to him in a manner calculated to entice him.

Darcy would not have minded where he was sitting, but the arrangement did not suit him at all, since he was too far from Elizabeth to have any opportunity to speak to her.

"Mr. Darcy, I wonder if I might exchange seats with you," said Mary.

"I would be happy to do," said Darcy.

Mrs. Bennet glared at Mary, who ignored her mother and smiled politely at Mr. Collins as she took her seat next to him.

"Mr. Collins, I have an excerpt I would like to discuss. I have written it down. It is from a philosophical text by..."

"How droll! Philosophy over breakfast?" said Lydia, with a bored pout, "surely even for *you* that is a bit too much, Mary."

"Not at all, Cousin Lydia," said Collins. "It is perfectly acceptable to begin the day with mental stimulation as well as physical."

Since everyone looked at him with varying degrees of dismay, he realized he had to explain what he meant.

"I was talking of food, of course."

He gave a little laugh, puffed up at his clever response.

From across the table, Elizabeth caught Darcy's eye and quirked her brow. Darcy made use of his napkin to hide his smile.

Meanwhile, politeness dictated he should engage in conversation with Miss Kitty on his left and Miss Mary on the right. However, he soon realized that both young ladies were more interested in joining the general conversation than talking to him, and he gave up.

A few minutes passed, and he began to feel at peace, allowing the ebb and flow of conversation to flow around him. Strangely enough, it was a relief to be ignored, and he found himself in harmony with Mr. Bennet, who was observing everything around him with detached amusement.

Then abruptly, Mr. Collins stood up with a loud scraping of his chair.

"I hope I may be excused, but I wonder if I could speak to Cousin Elizabeth in private?"

Darcy felt suddenly sick. The baked eggs he just ate were like pebbles in his stomach. He would have to put a stop to this. He could not allow Collins to steal Elizabeth from right under his nose. He stood up, struggling against the urge to plant a facer on Collins' self-satisfied little face.

Then several things happened. Lydia dropped her spoon into her bowl of gruel, splashing the contents across the table and onto Mr. Collins' coat.

"Look what you have done, Lydia!" said Mary. "You have ruined Mr. Collins' beautiful coat. Come with me, Mr. Collins, I will sort this out for you."

Collins glared at Lydia, then stared down at his

coat in dismay.

Mary clucked reassuringly. "Now, Mr. Collins, there is no need to be disturbed. We will take care of it in the blink of an eye."

Meanwhile Elizabeth had jumped to her feet as well.

"I am sorry, Mr. Collins, but I just remembered I left my bonnet in the garden. I had better fetch it before it starts to rain."

Collins was too preoccupied with his coat to answer. He went along with Mary, who coaxed him out of the breakfast room.

"Yes, yes," said Mrs. Bennet, waving her handkerchief and looking distressed. "Go fetch your bonnet quickly, child. Mary, come back! I can feel a spasm coming on."

Darcy came to his feet as well. Elizabeth had offered him a golden opportunity. He would follow her into the garden.

Mr. Bennet cleared his throat and stood up.

"Before you all go off in different directions, I hope at least one of you is willing to see me off. I will be departing for Gloucestershire in a few minutes."

No one paid Mr. Bennet any attention. Elizabeth went out without a backward glance; Mrs. Bennet was standing in the hallway, waving her handkerchief, and calling for Lydia to go after Mary and *do* something; and Jane was sneaking off with Bingley to find a moment of privacy. Only Kitty remained seated at the table.

Not for long. She took up a forkful of food and jammed it into her mouth, then pushed her plate and went to chase after Lydia.

"Well then," said Mr. Bennet with a sardonic smile. "That seemed to have done the trick. I have cleared the room. I was feeling a headache coming on, with all that caterwauling."

He bowed to Mr. Darcy.

"And now by your leave, I will begin my journey in that luxurious carriage of yours."

Darcy bowed politely.

"I hope you have a safe journey, and I am sorry for your loss."

Mr. Bennet nodded his thanks and left the room. As he disappeared, it occurred to Darcy that he had not asked Mr. Bennet's permission to marry Elizabeth. Mr. Bennet would not be back for several days.

Darcy did not hesitate. He caught up with Mr. Bennet as his valise was being loaded onto the carriage.

"Before you leave, sir, if I might have a moment of your time?"

Mr. Bennet sent him a quizzical look.

"Very well, Mr. Darcy. I can spare you a moment, but no more. I have already been delayed enough by the theatrics this morning. We can talk in the library."

Mr. Bennet led the way to the library. After they

had entered, he shut the door, locked it, and stood with his hat balanced on his cane, waiting for Darcy to speak. He did not offer the younger man a seat.

Darcy was taken aback. This was not how Darcy had envisioned asking permission for a lady's hand in marriage.

Mr. Bennet's eyes glinted with amusement.

"Do not expect we will have our privacy for long," he said, again showing an uncanny ability to read his mind. "You will have to say your piece quickly before we are interrupted."

"I wanted to take this opportunity—"

The was a loud banging on the door.

"Mr. Bennet! You must come at once!"

A satirical expression crossed the older man's face.

"I knew it," he said, with an exaggerated sigh. "If only I did not have such accurate powers of prediction."

He wagged his brows at Mr. Darcy.

"I will be with you shortly, Mrs. Bennet," he said loudly. "I am currently engaged with Mr. Darcy."

He turned to Darcy.

"I would recommend you to be very brief, sir. We are running out of time."

When Darcy had conceived of asking Elizabeth to marry him, he had conjured up the perfect romantic moment. Never in his wildest dreams did he imagine such mayhem. If this was a taste of what his married life would be, then heaven help him.

"Mr. Bennet!" came Mrs. Bennet's voice. "You cannot hide in there forever."

Mr. Bennet looked towards Darcy. "You heard what Mrs. Bennet said. The clock is ticking."

There was nothing for it. The time for finesse was over.

"Mr. Bennet," he said, in the simplest way possible, "May I request your permission to address Miss Elizabeth?"

"You may address her as much as you wish, Mr. Darcy. You do not need my permission."

The casual response suggested that Mr. Bennet had not understood his meaning.

"I beg your pardon, sir, but I did not make myself clear. I meant to say that I would like to ask for Elizabeth's hand in marriage."

"Ah. I am happy to hear you have finally come round to it. I assume your finances are all in order, that you have discharged all your gambling debts honorably, and you are not about to be thrown in the debtor's jail for unpaid bills?"

Darcy was thrown completely off guard. He did not know whether to take exception or to laugh.

"Everything is in order, sir."

"And you are prepared to sign a generous settlement?"

"Naturally."

"Good. I trust you are a man of your word. Then you have my blessings."

"Are you not curious to know if I love your daughter?"

"That is for you and Lizzy to sort out."

Mr. Bennet took his top hat from its perch on the cane and plunked it firmly on his head. With a finger to his lips, he unlocked the door, careful to make no sound.

"I would appreciate it if you could distract Mrs. Bennet while I can get away."

"But sir—"

"I am sure you will find a way, Mr. Darcy. Use your imagination. I would suggest falling to the ground in a faint. That always succeeds in drawing attention."

And with that, Mr. Bennet sneaked out through the servant's entrance, leaving Darcy to handle Mrs. Bennet.

∞∞∞

Luckily for Darcy, Mrs. Bennet ploughed past him as soon as he opened the door, searching for her husband. He had already left the room, and Mrs. Bennet did not even glance in Darcy's direction before running out to waylay him before the carriage left.

Darcy, trusting that Mr. Bennet could take care of himself, looked out of the window to see if he could spot Elizabeth outside.

He located her sitting on the swing, a book in her hand, completely indifferent to the pandemonium that had broken out inside.

He smiled.

Even if she was not waiting for him, he would not allow this opportunity to slip through his fingers.

He approached her with trepidation. Now that it came down to it, he did not have the slightest inkling if she had any feelings for him. In the maze, when he had kissed her, he had felt she might, but she pushed him away so quickly he may have imagined it.

She looked up as he approached, the crunching of the gravel alerting her.

"Is the furor over yet?"

He shook his head, unable to answer, caught by the mischievous laughter dancing over her lips.

"Has Mama sent you to fetch me? Because I swear, if she wants me to marry Mr. Collins now, I will —"

There was only one sure way to know how she felt, he thought. He took hold of the ropes of the swing and pulled Elizabeth towards him. The wet rope soaked through his gloves, but he ignored it.

"Mr. Darcy—" she sputtered.

His lips sank down into hers. As they connected, he felt a shudder that reached into his very soul. His need for her demanded more, but he forced himself to be gentle. He savored the moment, taking his time to woo her, giving her time to make up her mind. He did not press her. He wanted to give her a chance to move away if she wanted to.

He held back, and he waited.

She was motionless. She was breathing fast, but her eyes were shut tight, and, apart from a small murmur, she did nothing to reciprocate. He began to despair. What if she did not love him? What if he was wrong?

Then finally, she gave a cry and sank her fingers into his curls, pulling his head down. Her lips pressed against his, asking, demanding, searching for his very soul. He leaned into her hungrily, an insatiable yearning about to cut loose.

Is it so very strange that I would wish the gentleman who is my husband to love me?

The words broke through the daze of desire. She deserved to know the answer. He dragged himself out of his drunken joy and into the real world. He had promised her nothing. He had not even told her he was planning to stay. He was appalled. No wonder she had hesitated.

A radiant blossom of hope bloomed inside him. She had returned his kiss, without asking anything in return.

He let go of the swing, releasing his hold on her.

She blinked at him in confusion, her lips swollen with passion.

"Elizabeth," he said, scarcely recognizing the jagged edge of his voice. "We need to talk. You had better get off that swing."

"I do not know why you are objecting to this swing Mr. Darcy," she answered, recovering quickly, turning playful. She looked adorably tousled. "I have found it extremely useful these last two days."

"I have something I would like to ask you, but I cannot go down on my knee if I am worried you might swing forward and kick me in the head."

Her eyes danced with mischief. "I am now even more convinced of its usefulness. It is an excellent weapon in case of unwanted proposals. If I had been on the swing last Wednesday when Mr. Collins proposed, I would have swung forward and put an end to the proposal, and we would have been spared all the agony of the last week." She chortled. "I promise not to swing forward, if you promise me that you will not be a clod and give me a rehearsed speech."

Bingley had been adamant about not preparing a proposal speech, and Darcy could now see why. It seemed the Bennet sisters preferred a more spontaneous approach.

He could only hope he would live up to it.

He went down on one knee. He felt the mud squelch under his pale pantaloons, but it was too late to worry about it, and he soldiered onwards, determined not to let it stop him.

"Miss Elizabeth, you must allow me to tell you how ardently I admire you and love you," he said.

The swing creaked and came quickly towards him, threatening to knock him down. He swiftly leaned sideways, moving out of the way just in time.

"That will not do at all, Mr. Darcy. It sounds like something you must have read in a book."

He felt wounded. He had meant every word.

"I did not read it in a book," he said hotly. "The words are very much my own. But I see you are determined to make fun of me."

"I am sorry," she said, trying not to laugh. "It is just that your clothes are full of mud. Look at your gloves. And your pantaloons."

He stood up and tried to brush off the dirt from his knee. He only succeeded on making his gloves even dirtier. In the end, he took the gloves off and threw them to the ground. It suited him to have his hands bare, in any case.

"I will not make any speeches, then, Elizabeth." He reached out and traced the outline of her jaw with the tips of his right fingers. "I have no right to ask anything of you. I have said some abominable things to you. When you accused me of behaving in an ungentlemanly manner, I thought I could never forgive you. But it was not long before I recognized that I deserved every accusation you flung at me."

He stopped and took a deep breath. "You are too

generous to trifle with me, dearest, loveliest Elizabeth. If your feelings are still what they were last week, tell me so at once. One word from you will silence me forever. I will ride away and never inflict my presence on you again."

Apparently he had said the right thing after all, because Elizabeth's expressive eyes grew dark with emotion.

"We have both said things we regret, and I hope we have learned something from them. I am still learning now. It is very difficult to express how one feels. At least, I am finding it difficult."

She was shy. His darling Elizabeth was turning shy! He wanted to throw back his head and laugh, but it had to be handled delicately.

"Just say what you feel," he prompted, gently. "Just tell me the truth. That is all I ask of you. Always."

She lowered her eyes. He could not see her face, but her ears were burning.

"Very well, Mr. Darcy. Then I will have to tell you that – I love you."

She looked straight at him then, and the love shining out of her eyes was everything he had ever longed for. His heart felt so full he was afraid he would unman himself and cry.

"Elizabeth Bennet," he murmured, through a voice choked with emotion, "will you then do me the honor of giving me your hand in marriage?"

She put out her hand. "I will give you my hand,

Mr. Darcy, and I will give you my heart and soul as well, if you will have them."

He took her hand and brought it to his lips, thinking what a priceless gift she had given him. No fortune was big enough to compete with it.

"I love you, Elizabeth. Ardently. Fervently. With every fiber of my being."

The swing came swinging towards him, but this time, Elizabeth jumped from it and threw her arms around him. He caught her and crushed her to him, his lips grasping hers, his hands greedy for the feel of her body against him. He had dreamt of this moment many times, but the dream was nothing to the reality of holding her and feeling her softness against him.

It was impossible to put into words the sense of joyful elation that was spreading over him, and he would be foolish to try.

There were many other ways of expressing his feelings, and he could not wait to explore every single one of them.

Sometime later—he had no idea when—the sound of voices intruded on his happiness. Elizabeth gave a little squeak, then shoved at Darcy's chest. He stepped backwards, struggling to recover his demeanor and face the world.

"Elizabeth? Where are you?"

"Darcy?"

The crunch of the gravel warned them that Jane and Mr. Bingley were coming in their direction.

Elizabeth drew back and, with a shaky laugh, embarked on a valiant attempt to make herself presentable. With a chuckle, Darcy pushed away her hands and took over the task himself. There was no possible way to disguise completely what had happened, but he tried his best.

By the time Jane and Bingley reached them, Darcy had managed to repair the worst of the damage.

"Oh, there you are, Lizzy," said Jane. "We have been looking for you everywhere. There has been such an uproar. Mama has fallen into a fit—"

She stopped suddenly, noticing Elizabeth's crumpled appearance.

"Oh." Her gaze darted from Elizabeth to Darcy, her brow wrinkling.

Mr. Bingley was not quite as circumspect. He took in the situation with a quick glance and grinned widely.

"Darcy, you dog! Do not tell me you have gone ahead and done it?"

"Done what, Lizzy?"

"Mr. Darcy and I are engaged to be married."

She was looking so deliciously happy that Darcy wanted to take her in his arms all over again.

"Oh, Lizzy! Oh! I am so happy for you. Now my happiness is complete!"

As the young women laughed and embraced, Bingley slapped Darcy on the back.

"I am delighted you finally saw sense, Darcy. I was afraid your lofty notions might prove too stubborn to overcome. Allow me to be the first to offer my congratulations."

"LIZZY!!"

They turned to see Mrs. Bennet hurtling towards them. "Lizzy, you must come at once!"

Darcy reached out for Elizabeth's hand, and, squeezing it reassuringly, he began to walk in Mrs. Bennet's direction.

"We had better go and tell your Mama. I do not know how she will take it, but at least she might leave off trying to marry Lydia to Mr. Collins, now that she has caught a much bigger fish."

"I would not describe you as a fish, Mr. Darcy. I think a whale might be more appropriate."

"A whale? I am not quite sure if that is an insult or a compliment."

"Well, it would make it far more difficult for Mama to reel you in."

Epilogue

As they approached Mrs. Bennet, Elizabeth began to hesitate about telling her Mama the news in the presence of Mr. Darcy. She had no way of predicting what Mrs. Bennet would say, and Elizabeth preferred to find out in a more private setting. She said something vague to Mr. Darcy about breaking the news quietly, and, with the new-found tact he had been developing recently, he held back and waited for Elizabeth to come and fetch him, while Bingley and Jane started to walk towards a copse of trees.

"Mama," said Elizabeth, intercepting Mrs. Bennet before she reached Darcy. "I have important news to convey to you, if you would please step inside the house."

"News? What news? I cannot imagine anything more important than Mr. Collins."

"It cannot wait," said Elizabeth, firmly.

Mrs. Bennet's eyes widened. She led the way into the parlor and shut the door, consumed by curiosity.

Elizabeth followed her. It was clear Mrs. Bennet

had no idea of the news she was about to impart, so seeing her mother's impatience, Elizabeth made the announcement as quickly as she could.

The effect on Mrs. Bennet was extraordinary. She sat quite still, unable to utter a syllable. Her astonishment was so extreme, she refused to believe it.

"This must be one of your Papa's strange ideas of a joke, Lizzy. You cannot fool me so easily."

"It is no joke, Mama. I am engaged to Mr. Darcy."

Mrs. Bennet peered closely at Elizabeth, who put on her sternest face, and hoped she looked too serious for Mama to doubt her.

It must have worked, because Mrs. Bennet looked alarmed. "But are you certain, Lizzy? Are you quite sure you want to marry such an odious man? You must not do it, just because of his fortune."

The irony of this statement did not escape Elizabeth, especially when she considered that Mrs. Bennet was perfectly content to sacrifice Elizabeth to Mr. Collins.

She laughed. "He is not odious, Mama. Far from it. And you must not talk about him that way anymore if he is to be my husband, Mama. I love him."

By now Mrs. Bennet was beginning to recover, and Elizabeth's assurances knocked everything else out of her head. She went around the room, exclaiming in astonishment, still unable to believe her daughter's great fortune.

"Good gracious! Mr. Darcy! Who would have

thought it? Oh, my sweetest Lizzy! How rich and how great you will be! What pin-money, what jewels, what carriages you will have! Jane's is nothing to it -- nothing at all. I am so pleased! Such a charming man! So handsome! So tall! Oh, my dear Lizzy! Please apologize to him for my having disliked him so much before. I hope he will overlook it. Dear, dear Lizzy! A house in town! Everything that is charming! Ten thousand a year! Oh, heavens! I shall go distracted."

Elizabeth glanced uneasily towards the door. She was very glad now that she had not made the announcement in Mr. Darcy's presence.

Mrs. Bennet's effusions continued for a while, then came to an abrupt stop.

"But what about Mr. Bennet? He must give his permission immediately! What if he refuses his consent? For very likely, he does not like Mr. Darcy at all, and you know how your father is when he takes a notion into his head! Mr. Darcy must go after him at once and obtain his permission."

"You must tell him yourself, Mama. He is outside."

Mrs. Bennet continued, too overcome to hear a word Elizabeth was saying.

"Oh, and tell him he must obtain a special license! You must and shall be married by a special license! Also, you must tell me what dish Mr. Darcy is particularly fond of, so I can have it made tomorrow. I must go up to tell the others, and inform Mr. Collins that you are taken. He will have to marry your sister now. Oh, is that not the most wonderful news!"

And she hurried out of the room.

∞∞∞

Darcy was waiting in the garden, expecting any minute for Mrs. Bennet to come out and congratulate him.

He was surprised to see Elizabeth emerge alone, with Mrs. Bennet running precipitously up the stairs. He wondered if Mrs. Bennet's dislike of him extended so far that she had objected strongly to the marriage.

"Did you tell your mama?" he asked with some trepidation. "How did she take it?"

Elizabeth broke out into a smile. "I do believe she is delighted, but she has her own way of showing it. What is your favorite meal, by the way? Mama wishes to know. So do I. Please do not tell me it is some elaborate meal that must be prepared by the best French chefs. I would advise you to stick to hearty country fare."

"Well then," he said. "Tell me what your favorite meal is, and I shall endeavor to like it, and say that it is my favorite as well."

Elizabeth was just opening her mouth to answer when she was interrupted by a wail. Lydia came running down the stairs, crying, with Mrs. Bennet and Kitty in tow.

"It is so unfair, Mama! You must put a stop to it at once! You will have to pretend to faint again."

"But my dear, I cannot do the same thing twice."

"You must think of something else, then, quickly. I will not let Mary marry Mr. Collins."

They ran into the parlor and shut the door.

Elizabeth looked at Mr. Darcy, worried that the scene would bring back bad memories, but his eyes were full of mirth.

"Stay here a moment," she said. "Let me discover what is going on."

She crept up the stairs as quietly as she could, avoiding the stair that tended to creak loudly.

The door to Mary's bedchamber was half open, and Mr. Collins was kneeling on one knee.

"—the violence of my affections," he was saying.

Afraid she was going to laugh out loud and interrupt Mr. Collins once again, she went back down to join Darcy.

"Well?" said Mr. Darcy. "Are they engaged?"

"Not yet. Mr. Collins has not completed his speech."

"Perhaps you should find a way to hurry them on."

"Fie, Mr. Darcy!" she replied, with a haughty quirk of her brow. "Surely you are not implying that I should employ *subterfuge?*" She gave him a beguiling smile that threw all other thoughts from his brain.

"Besides, I can think of far better ways to spend my time."

She pulled him into the house and down the corridor to the breakfast room. She shut the door.

"Now, where were we, before Bingley and Jane interrupted?" she murmured, coming closer to him and rising on her tiptoes.

"I do not recall exactly," said Darcy, his mouth going dry. "You might wish to remind me."

"With pleasure, Mr. Darcy."

She slid her fingers through his curls and pulled herself towards him, and then he forgot everything else.

THE END

∞ ∞ ∞

If you enjoyed this book by Monica Fairview, please support the author by leaving a review.

You can sign up to receive news and exclusive previews on Monica's blogs:

Website: darcyregencynovels.com
Blog: austenvariations.com

Other Books by Monica Fairview

Variations

> Dangerous Magic
> Fortune and Felicity
> Mysterious Mr. Darcy
> The Darcy Brothers

Comedy

> Mr. Darcy's Pledge
> Mr. Darcy's Challenge
> Mr. Darcy's Pride and Joy

Sequels

> The Other Mr. Darcy: Miss Bingley's Tale
> The Darcy Cousins: Miss Darcy Finds Love

Quirky

> Steampunk Darcy: Inspired by Jane Austen

Regency

> An Improper Suitor
> An Unexpected Duke
> Dancing Through the Snow
> A Merry Christmas Chase

About Monica Fairview

Monica Fairview writes Jane Austen sequels and variations as well as Regencies. Her biggest claim to fame is living in Elizabeth Gaskell's house in Manchester, long before the house was restored. After studying in the USA, she taught literature, then became an acupuncturist. She now lives near London.

Apart from her avid interest in the 19th century, Monica enjoys reading fantasy and post-apocalyptic novels, but avoids zombies like the plague. She loves to laugh, drink tea, and visit National Trust Properties, and she is convinced that her two cats can understand everything she says.

To sign up to receive the latest about Monica's news and new releases, please visit

Website: darcyregencynovels.com
Blog: austenvariations.com

Printed in Great Britain
by Amazon